GAMBLE
ON MURDER

THE SECOND CONNER MILES MYSTERY

STEVEN D. MALONE

Gamble on Murder
The Second Conner Miles Mystery

Copyright © 2021 Steven D. Malone

by Steven D. Malone

ISBN: 978-1-7338839-1-7

TABLE OF CONTENTS

THE BOX

November 1925

Sometimes your destiny stares you in the face and you don't know it.

My longtime partner, Bobbie Lee Glover, and I spent the morning in labor. Well, doing labor. Helped a bunch of guys lug furniture into a solid-built house a couple of blocks up from the Seawall. A one story place, thank God. Still, as required by city ordinance, it sat high on brick pilings. The hope was to keep it up high, out of any hurricane's storm surge. The long climb up its stairway made me appreciate the chill breeze that blew in from Galveston Bay.

Tall, though not quite as tall as me, movie star handsome Sam Maceo had me watching the others since lunch. Black hair to my brunette. Sicilian coloring to my pasty Irish. Bolder nose than mine. Lips fuller than mine. Tailored, dark green suit to my off-the-shelf ash gray. Double breasted, dark blue overcoat to my well-worn, dull brown flogger. Black wool Homburg pressed firmly on his head. My Fedora still lay in the Studebaker.

With his easy grin, stark glint, and suave manner, Sam was an up-and-coming lieutenant of the Beach Gang. My Gang. He was also the brother of Rosario (Rose) Maceo. My boss.

A loud thud sounded from the truck. Shouts too, as Bobbie Lee and the other men wrestled a poker table from it.

"Mr. Glover," Sam said. Not a loud call, but it froze everyone in their places. "Gently. Don't bruise it."

"Yessir, Mr. Maceo. We'll do better. Promise," Bobbie Lee said.

"Nice enough place, you think?" Sam asked me.

I had my teeth clenched together to stop their chattering, but I managed. "Very nice, Mr. Maceo."

"It's yours, Conner."

"Mine?"

"Well, yours to use. Your reward."

"Reward?"

"Yes. For cleaning up that mess last summer." Sam favored me with one of his winning smiles.

I felt the two hundred and something dollars rolled and stuffed in my pants pocket. All that was left of a grand. "Mr. Maceo, your brother paid me for that months ago."

"That was for the job. You did the job," he said. "But you bought us a lot more, you see?"

That job, as he called it, was running down a murderer. A can of worms got opened along the way. And, like a line of dominoes, events fell out so that the pockets of the Maceo brothers and the Beach Gang got lined.

"I don't know what to say." Mostly because I still had no idea what Sam was telling me. All I was doing was moving furniture into an empty house.

Sam saw the puzzle on my mug. He laughed his smooth laugh.

"We're giving you a game. Poker. Not high roller but not low roller. It's yours though."

My jaw dropped.

He smiled that smile again. "We get our cut. But the game is yours."

"Damn, Mr. Maceo." I had no other words. What the hell did I know about running a poker game?

"Don't worry, Conner. You get some help."

"God, I hope so."

"You get your own crew."

"Crew?"

Sam nodded over to the men helping Bobbie Lee. "That's them. So, from now on, start bossing and stop sweating."

He stuck a thumb and forefinger to his lips and blew a shrill whistle. With a gesture, he drew them all over to the two of us. Bobbie Lee, always looking like a boy dressed in his daddy's clothes, and the three others gathered. None of them looked all that tough as they hunched against the cold wind.

"Boys, this is Conner. He's your new number one. That youngster," Sam pointed a finger at Bobbie Lee. "He's your number two."

The three guys looked surprised. Maybe as surprised as I was. As Bobbie Lee was.

"You've been part of the Beach," Sam continued. The Beach, that's what we called ourselves. Not the Beach Gang. That's what the newspapers and the law called us. "So you know what's expected. What Rose and I, and Ollie Quinn expect. You follow?"

Ollie Quinn was the boss of the Beach Gang.

Sam waited. Finally it dawned on them that some kind of an answer was expected.

"Yessir. Yes, Mr. Maceo."

My new crew may not have been the sharpest set of gangsters in town, I was thinking.

Sam turned to me. "I'll leave you with it while you're still too stunned to thank me."

"Uh, thank you, Mr. Maceo." Could I have been more dunderheaded?

Sam chuckled all the way to his brown-on-tan Packard.

"Slap my bottom and call me Nancy," Bobbie Lee marveled. "But ain't we got it made."

I turned away from watching the Packard disappear down the road. "Not yet we don't. Now that we have whatever we have, we gotta make it work."

Bobbie Lee gave me a shy smile beneath his blond curls.

"What?" I asked him.

"Worried?"

"You bet. This is all new territory, Bobbie Lee. I don't know what I'm doing." Thinking about it made the day seem colder.

"The Maceo's are giving us a step up," he said. "And you can do it."

Could I? My baby-faced, longtime partner placed a whole batch of faith in me. Faith in something I knew nothing about. "I guess we better get started. Figure out what's next."

The inside of the house was even better than the outside. The large front room spread all the way to the back of the house. There, French doors opened onto stairs leading to what looked like a winter-worn patio garden. A well-appointed kitchen on the right. Bedrooms and bath on the left.

"What a skirt I am." Bobbie Lee grinned. "I'm already picturing what we can do with the place. A little bar over on the right. A table by the back where we can count the money..."

"Already got us making money, huh?"

"Figure Rose will be expecting us to."

"You mean Mr. Maceo?" I teased. A man didn't want to get in the habit of calling his boss by his first name. Especially not a boss like Rose Maceo.

"Sorry. I gotta watch myself." He cracked a boyish smile.

Our crew, all three of them in a bunch, came stomping in from the back of the house somewhere. They got all wide-eyed when they spotted us. I guessed they were as uncomfortable as the two of us at the new arrangement.

"We moved that couch and that lounge chair back in the den. Hope that's all right," the chubby redhead said through a face full of freckles.

"Why not?" I shrugged. "What's your name?"

"Joey Books."

"Like to read, do you?"

His turn to shrug. "Not really."

"Then why do they call you that?"

"Because I'm a Jew. Joseph Buchman. What else are they gonna call me?"

I looked at him a second. Didn't think he was all that pleased with his nickname.

"How about Joe?" I asked.

Joe's grin widened. Got that one right.

"What are we going to do with the place, Joe?"

He looked at me, as stumped as I was, I thought.

"I know what you are going to do, Conner."

I turned to find Dianne Starr standing in my doorway. Dianne Starr, the Handmaiden. Ex-prostitute, brothel owner, and a five-foot two pack of pure dynamite. Short petite, blond, and marked with a crimson birthmark on her right cheek. Black wool skirt. Black wool overcoat with a silver fox fur collar. For whatever reason, she counted me a friend and I hoped she knew how much I appreciated the friendship.

"Well, I'm glad someone does," I said.

She smiled. "You're going to nurse a bunch of marks as they empty their pockets across that misplaced gaming table."

"Yessss, ma'am."

"Don't ma'am me. I bought a surprise or two." Dianne gestured behind her to things in the yard I couldn't see.

A moment later her friend—her special friend—I knew as Contrary Mary, entered, hauling in two large paintings. Behind her, more women followed carrying more paintings.

Contrary Mary, handsome with her boyish hair bob, wore a man's suit and a bitter frown. Tall, taciturn, Mary had a reputation as a knife fighter. No one wanted to be cut by Contrary Mary. In a cottony contralto, she directed the women here and there with the paintings.

Dianne reached to push the button. The overhead chandelier flicked on. Well, the two bulbs still working did. One bulb flickered like it was haunted.

"We'll have to do something about that," she said, making dubious eyes at the lights. "We could use some help. There's more out in Mary's truck."

I looked over to the knot of boys goggling at Dianne's friends bending to lean their art work against the walls.

"Hey," I called. "Go help."

That made them jump. Bobbie Lee, too. Contrary Mary found herself leading a parade out into the chill.

"I knew the minute I heard, that you know nothing about what needs doing."

I shook my head. "You know right, I'm afraid. And, I'd owe you for any help you offer."

"It's offered. Got any tools around here?"

"No idea."

"Maybe Mary has some out in her truck." She took off her coat and draped it across a chair. "First thing we have to do is put that table where it ought to go."

The two of us lugged the table closer to the kitchen and away from the fireplace. The chairs followed then we watched. Contrary Mary directed as my crew returned the couch and lounge chair to the room and the women hammered nails and hung pictures.

I wasn't sure about having pictures on the wall. Especially art chosen by women. Didn't expect anyone but men coming in for a game. But Dianne chose well. Landscapes, mostly, of ranch land and stark, rocky hills.

"Out west, looks like," I said, letting my eyes roam across the walls.

"Off west of San Antonio, I suspect. The man that did 'em is from there."

"Impressive, Dianne. Starting to look like a proper reward," I said.

She made a face. "Is that what Rose told you?"

"Sam told me that."

"That sounds like Sam," she said. She waved a hand across the room. "What you really got is a job. You know that, don't you?"

All of a sudden the room looked different.

"He'll expect you to make him some money."

"Yeah. He will, won't he." It was not a question.

"What's the matter? You people don't believe in paying your gas bill?"

A tall, willow of a woman leaned against the opened door, arms crossed under her breasts, sandy hair uncovered, and wearing a pale blue outfit, blouse, cardigan and pleated skirt. No jacket.

"My other surprise. Come in, girl." Dianne beamed. "Meet Conner."

The woman straightened and marched up to me on the longest set of legs I'd seen in a while.

I stood into her green eyes and broad grin. She had to be a thumb's width taller than me and had a strong, Texas handshake.

"Glad to meet you. I'm Jennifer. Jenny."

"Jenny's a mechanic," Dianne said.

"Mechanic?"

"I deal cards, darlin'." Jenny said. "Still haven't told me why it's so cold in here."

"Let me see what I can do," I promised.

Somewhere along the way, someone had run a gas line through the fireplace and attached it to a space heater. The thing was huge and looked like a cast iron park bench with a bank of fire bricks set along its back. I found a box of kitchen matches on the mantel. The heater hissed to life and I cranked it up full blast.

"The beautiful, the courageous, Gen-Gen, assistant to Kalil the Magnificent. Magi of Araby. Luminous keeper of the Ancient Scrolls of the Secret Eye. Hypnotist and Magician to all the Royalty of Europe and Asia," Dianne nearly sang.

"Good God, woman. Enough," Jenny said. "I can't believe you still remember that bilge."

"Circus act?" I asked.

"Circus. Vaudeville. Burlesque. If there was a limelight glowing, Hiram'd do his show."

"Hiram?"

"Hiram Schwarzer, the Magnificent Kalil. Bless him." Jenny's eyes welled.

"Hiram passed four or five years back," Dianne explained. "Left Jenny stranded here. Liked it enough to stay, I guess."

"And no, I didn't," Jenny challenged.

"Didn't what?"

"Work the houses. I played piano or flute over at the Opera House. Danced if it wasn't pure ballet. Even sang a little."

"Now Jenny, Conner's the last of the gentlemen. He wouldn't imply such a thing. He'd think it maybe. But he wouldn't say it," Dianne teased.

"That's unfair, Dianne," I said. Anyway, it wouldn't have mattered to me if she whored. A girl had to make her way in the world.

The two women shared the glance all women share when they're rousting a man. I puffed a loud sigh.

"So youngster, you're setting up a game?" Jenny asked.

"I got this house, this table, these chairs," I answered.

"That's all?" Jenny's eyes widened.

"I bet I know," Bobbie Lee called from the hallway. He raised up a finger, wanting us to wait, then disappeared into a back room.

He wobbled back in, his top half hidden by a sizable wooden crate. He managed to put it down between Jenny and me. Its top popped off easy enough.

"Excellent." Jenny smiled. "There's your box and your chips."

I would've called it a chip tray, so I learned something. The chips lay beneath, scattered loosely in a disorganized pile. Jenny stirred through them."

"Oh look, cards. Sealed packs," she said. "Not enough, though. You need to get more."

I marveled. There had to be thirty, forty packs.

"More?"

"Gamblers are a suspicious, and superstitious bunch, Conner," Dianne put in. "They'll want new ones if they get to thinking their luck turned."

Jenny pulled out a deck and tore the seal. In a couple of seconds, she began to do magician's flourishes and some sleight-of-hand tricks. Never a glance at them. Not to show off, I thought, but to practice. Amazing.

She looked at me. "Made any plans at all?"

"I thought about putting in a bar. Maybe over there." I pointed back over my shoulder.

"Drinks gonna cost your marks?"

I shook my head. "No."

"Get somebody good for when you get some mark on a tilt. And you will."

"On a tilt?"

"A string of bad luck that makes the mark all angry. A drink, a smile, encouraging words. Somebody to calm 'im down."

Sounded like good sense. "I'll look around."

"You got a brush or two?" Jenny asked. She started to cut the deck of cards, one-handed. Measured me with her gaze.

"A brush?"

The two women exchanged a glance.

"The Paddy doesn't know a thing about this. Why did Rose set him up?" Jenny asked.

"Rose likes him. For some reason." Dianne grinned. "Expects him to be an earner."

That was a nice surprise. Earners ran the Gang businesses. That would keep me out of enforcing and such like. Out of the more dangerous jobs being a part of this thing of ours. I still didn't like being talked about like I'd left the room.

"Teach me then. What the hell's a brush?"

Another one of those "knowing" glances women do when they get something over a man. Though I betted that Dianne didn't know either.

"Some folks, well-placed, that'll steer marks to your game," Jenny said. She turned to Dianne. "You have some of those around town, I bet."

"I don't call them that, but I do."

"Bellboys. A bartender or two, here and there, yes?"

"A couple or so—here or there." Dianne nodded. "But he'll have to get his own. I'm not sharing."

"I'll take care of it," I huffed into the quirk of a smile. How, I didn't know. Yet.

"Nothing stopping you from making your own, Conner." Jenny said. "Some men might want a tumble, some might want a game. Give some boys a little juice, and they'll send folks your way."

I'd of given her a thank you—sort of—but Contrary Mary came in to whisper in Dianne's ear. The woman's smirking smile went away.

"I have to leave." She stood.

"Trouble?" I asked.

"Meh, it's always turmoil and drama among my girls." Dianne turned to Jenny, questions on her mug.

"I think I'll stay. Teach these boys more about my favorite game. Don't let your drama follow you around," Jenny said.

"Will try," Dianne said over her shoulder as she followed Mary out the door.

"Poker's not your game, huh, Conner?" Jenny said, two days later. She fanned the deck of cards in a long arc in front of her.

"No, it's not," I answered.

She watched me a minute. "Tell me? Why not?"

"You've seen me play these last couple of days." I grinned. "I've got more tells on my mug than the front page of the newspaper, and you know it."

Jenny laughed. A full, rich laugh. A strong laugh. I liked it.

"I do," she said. "And it's good that *you* know it."

"Kept my change in my pockets, I figure."

Her hands swooped up the fanned deck and a couple of taps squared it up. She shuffled it, then began to cut the deck several times. She held it up before me. A single card rose out of it as if by magic. It fell onto the table. Ace of Clubs.

Jenny cut it again. Another card did its levitation and fell. Ace of Diamonds.

Another cut. Another card. Ace of Hearts.

Once more. Ace of Spades.

"You're sure you want to play it straight up? Honest games?" she asked.

"That's what I want," I answered. "You'll be dealing, not playing."

"The rake okay?"

The rake, our rake, gave us our income. We'd take a dribble for the house on each hand dealt.

"A dollar per player, per hand. Five-dollar ante." I nodded. "That is, if you think we'll make money?"

"Oh, we ought to do all right. Cover the bills." Jenny shrugged. "The place is shaping up."

I looked around. We'd been busy during the day. The lamps and fixtures all had new light bulbs. Food in the refrigerator and cabinets. Bobbie Lee found something he said was a "Cortina Credenza" with a marble top. We ripped the back off of it, stuck it in the front right corner by the kitchen door, and stuffed it with liquor and glasses. Our bar.

Someone knocked on the door. Bobbie Lee and Joey Books—Joe— trotted in from the back of the house.

They opened the door to find Rose Maceo, with a handful of men and a slip of an Asian girl. I didn't know the men, but the girl was Mai.

Mai whored independently but often showed up at Dianne Starr's place. Bobbie Lee and I knew her from before, and she counted Bobbie Lee as a friend. She always giggled and smiled like she was ten, but her dark eyes held wisdom as old as Eve.

Rose Maceo looked for all the world like the small town barber he'd once been.

A rough-cut, round face. A touch stocky. Quick to smile and shake a hand. His baritone voice rolled through a South Louisiana accent undercut by thick Italian inflections. Where his smooth, handsome brother, Salvatore (Sam) shone like a movie star, Rose was gravel rough and snake ruthless. I blessed my luck that, for whatever reason, the man liked me.

He brushed by Mai, and let the men inside. Mai smiled that little girl smile and scruffed Bobbie Lee's blond curls.

"We early, Conner?" Rose asked, not really caring if they were. "Look at dis place. Good job."

"Thank you, Mr. Maceo."

"Boys, dis is da' Conner. Dis is his game." Rose began ushering them toward the table. I noticed he thickened his Cajun accent. Something he often did if he didn't want to appear as sharp as he was.

Christ on a crutch, the man intended us to start tonight. We weren't ready.

I shot a panicked glance at Jenny. She returned an almost invisible shrug. Bobbie Lee's shrug—not so much.

He followed the men to the table. "Your hats, please. What's everybody drinking?"

Thanked God for Bobbie Lee, I did. Because I hadn't thought of that.

"Conner," Rose called. Maybe to rescue me.

I went over to him. "Yessir?"

"You *are* ready, Conner," he told me softly.

"Friday. Friday was to be the first game." I wanted this game. I wanted it to work. For me, and for Rosario Maceo.

"Dis is ready." He gestured around the room. "How would you be more ready come Friday, cher."

Rose pronounced it as "shah."

Jenny counted out chips. Mai poured drinks with a focused smile, without even being asked. Bobbie Lee, done with the hats, cranked up the Victrola.

"Well, looks like the place works," I told Rose. He had to hear the surprise in my voice.

"Deez men, dey belong to some high rollers in town. Sam has 'em up in the Hotel Galvez."

"Showing them a good time?"

Rose smiled. "Dat and to do 'em some business. Now you go do your job. Keep your eyes opened."

"Yessir."

He shut the door on the way out.

I walked, eyes opened, to stand behind Jenny and faced my players and their stacks of chips.

"…game is poker. Draw or stud." She flashed a silver dollar. "This button'll spot who opens. That man can call the game. Left of him cuts."

"We get a high/low with the stud?" One of the marks asked.

One of the three businessman types. I guessed a banker, by the look of him. The fourth man was pure gangster. He'd look like nothing else, even without that pistol bulge beneath his jacket.

"Well, if you want to play children's games, it'd be your call." Jenny softened that with a mischievous smirk. "Be ready. The house takes a rake. A dollar per player, per hand dealt. I'll announce it. Are we ready to play?

They all nodded.

"Five-dollar ante. All horses to the gates," she announced.

MARKS

———————————⟨⟩⟨◉⟩⟨⟩———————————

What should I have called the marks? Not marks. Not in front of them. Customers? Clients? Players? They played well as far as I could tell. Slow and steady. Serious, beneath the blue cloud of cigar smoke.

The banker type, in his black pinstriped suit, wore the best poker face. Solid and firm, with a half-smile, turning up the edges of his mouth, and never a flicker or twitch in his pale blue eyes. In the brief snatches of conversation, it turned out that he made a living financing construction companies. So, was that something like a banker?

The man next to him, whose veiny, red nose predicted that he would be swallowing most of my bourbon, played the loosest and bluffed the most.

My pistol-packing gangster, Tony, figured red nose out fairly early, calling him on it time and time again. It didn't always work. One of the man's best bluffs was that sometimes he wasn't bluffing. Tony would throw down his cards and lay a match to a fat cigar that hadn't always gone out.

The last man at the table said little and played his game close to the vest. I never really knew the meaning of that term until that night, seeing him pull his cards up against his chest and turning them out at the corners to peek quickly at his hand. His shifty eyes always on the watch for Bobbie Lee and Joe, and where they were in the room. On the lookout for a turn of the head or a shift in the chairs of the other players. He was generally the first to fold and rarely raised, no matter how good a hand. That he ever called was his tell. If he stayed in, he had a good hand.

"Pair of sevens," Tony grinned after calling the bluffer.

The bluffer just shook his head and threw his cards down.

My banker's lips turned down in a rare frown. He'd folded earlier and I'd give even money he had better than two sevens.

"You mean I won? Well, damn," Tony said and scooped in the scattering of chips. Before stacking them, he tossed in a five dollar chip. "I'm in. Let's go."

Jenny smiled. "Eager, are we? Who else?"

She started shuffling as the others threw in their ante. The button sat in front of the drinker. She placed the deck in front of Mister Close-to-the-vest. I counted. The man cut the deck four times.

"Give me something better than a couple of sevens, darling," Close-to-the-vest said to Jenny.

Jenny smiled. "Want a new deck?"

He shook his head. "Doubt if it'd help."

"No, no, no," the drinker said. "Lot o' luck in this deck."

"Didn't help you last time," Tony said.

"It's gonna this time," the drinker said. He straightened his hand and took a drink. "Let me show you. Sight unseen."

The man dropped twenty dollars in chips into the pot.

That earned him a host of hard stares.

"Well, this'll be entertaining," Jenny said, passing me a bemused glance. She dropped a dollar chip into the pot and removed a five. "House rake. Who's in?"

The banker pulled his cards up for a study. "All right. I'll see it and I got twenty more. That'll sure separate the fool from his money."

"See it and twenty more on top, to do the same thing." Tony grinned as he dropped chips onto the table.

Close-to-the-vest pressed his cards to his belly for a peek. His eyes shifted from his cards to Drinker and back again several times. Often enough to earn an impatient grimace from Tony.

"That's sixty to me to stay in this parade?" he asked Jenny who nodded. He put in his chips. He must've had good cards. "You gonna look yet?"

Drinker knew the man's tells well enough by now.

"Yessir. Yessir, I think I will this time," Drinker said.

The bastard took a look, then saw the bet. Another bluff? Lots of chips lay scattered on the table.

"This is fun, gentlemen. Who wants cards," Jenny asked. Her eyes watched Drinker.

Not a twitch. Not a blink. He pulled a single card. Jenny flicked me a wink. She had a pretty smile. One off the top went over to him.

The Banker's eyes never left Drinker as he pushed cards over to Jenny. "Give me two."

"I don't believe you filled that house," Tony said, giving a broad grin to Close-to-the-vest. "In fact, I figure that pretty lady'll give me another pair to chase my aces. Won't 'cha, pretty lady?"

He laid down three cards, hoping for a second pair. And maybe an ace or face card kicker. He waited to look at them until Close-to-the-vest drew three cards as well. Drinker fanned out his hand, as if to consider them one more time. Didn't. He pushed them back together. Not a twitch. Not a blink. His fingers pinched three twenty-dollar chips from his stack. They dropped one at a time, in a line, at the edge of the disheveled pile.

"If you want to see them…" Drinker started. He didn't have to finish.

One of the man's bluffs. Which kind?

"God damn, James," the Banker said quietly. "God damn."

Now I knew the Drinker's name. James. James didn't twitch. James didn't blink. He just stared at the pile of chips in the pot.

I stared too.

Jenny gave me a nudge with her elbow. "Five hundred, less our four dollars.

"Think we need a bigger rake?" I chuckled. It looked like we'd have a good night.

She shrugged then rolled those green eyes. "Next time. Maybe."

"Maybe."

"Here's my sixty," the Banker said. "You don't have it.

His eyes shifted past Jenny to pistol-toting Tony. I should've said something to Bobbie Lee about that thing. Probably didn't have to. Bobbie Lee and Joe were standing now. Watching the play. Even Mai leaned her elbows on the bar to see.

Bobbie Lee flicked me a look. He made to rebutton his jacket. Opening it, closing it, and buttoning it again. In the process he flashed the pistol sticking in his waist. Flashed it to show me he was ready.

Tony tapped his cards with a finger as he contemplated James. After a moment he grinned and tossed in his chips.

"You better be able to best aces," he said.

"You're called." Close-to-the-vest tossed in his chips.

James swallowed the last of his whiskey. "Well, I gotta pair of Jacks and a couple of threes."

"Ha, you bluffing bastard. Look at these three eights," Tony crowed. He slammed down his hand. Three eights, sure enough."

"What? Not aces?" The Banker shook his head. Down came his cards. Face down. "Couldn't beat three eights. A sad day, some days," James said. "Especially on the day I flop down that third three."

Which he did. He had filled that Full House. I eyed Tony carefully. Weighing my chances of grabbing his pistol before he shot anyone. The gat stayed tucked under his arm, but his stare could have killed.

As my players turned in chips for cash, I walked my sore feet over to a chair next to Bobbie Lee. Jenny sat sorting and stacking chips back into the box.

Murray Spats waited by the door. Spats ranked high in Ollie Quinn's crew of top guys. A sign of Ollie's regard for the assortment of visitors. Murray might not have worn his spats that night, but he served as driver, taking my players back to their hotels.

"Nice night, Conner. Have me back, okay?" The Banker said as he slipped his winnings into his coat pocket.

"Come knock. I'll open the door," I said.

Bobbie Lee grinned. "Actually, I'll be opening the door, but we'll be happy to see all y'all again."

That was his job, one of them. I gave a wave. Spats herded them out.

"You didn't mind me opening my stupid mouth, did you?" Bobbie Lee asked.

I shook my head, then arched a warning eyebrow. "Sometimes I might, though."

Maybe he heard me.

"Looks like we had a good first night." He patted the stacks of bills that sat near the chessboard he and Joe played on through most of the night.

Two stacks, even-steven. One for us. One for Rose Maceo.

I agreed, though I wished the stacks lay a touch higher.

"Smile, Conner. We are on our way." Bobbie Lee grinned. My baby-faced friend lit up like a flash pan.

I met Bobbie Lee when I joined up with a crew of bootleggers back in the Fall of 1921. He stayed with me when our crew got run out of Arkansas. We hustled nickels and dimes on the streets of Galveston for too long a time. Rose Maceo took us off those streets to bootleg liquor on the west end beaches.

"What are you gonna do with all that money?" I fluttered the stack of bills. By the time I paid off the crew, covered the next order of liquor, and whatever else, his share should be about twenty-eight bucks. Two weeks wages for most people.

"Boy, that's a question." Bobbie Lee stared upwards and considered. "I think I'll buy a new knife. Maybe take Mai over to Trudeau's for some gumbo."

My friend did like his steel and gumbo that tasted like Archangel Michael stewed it up himself. I didn't worry about his tangling with Mai. The world's happiest whore through and through, Mai was. Beautiful inside and out. But, from all I could see, he was in it for the fun. So was she. And he didn't lose his smile or brood when Mai plied her trade. Didn't pimp her, either. The woman bossed herself.

"What you gonna do with your share, Conner?" Joe asked. He arranged the chessmen for a new game.

I shook my head. "No idea. Haven't thought about it. Not once."

Not true. I'd put myself to sleep nights thinking of little else. Just didn't want to hex anything by saying it out loud.

"You know the Paddy lies," Jenny said. She dropped the chip box a couple of times on the table. Her way of settling them. She placed it just so before coming to sit on my other side.

She patted my knee. "You did good tonight."

"I didn't do anything." I did, however, feel a warm kind of shadow of that touch most of the rest of the night.

"Sorry, my friend, you did everything. You had a game waiting. You stood tall, looking like every bit the Paddy gangster." Jenny gestured across me to Bobbie Lee and Joe. "You had your crew sitting close. You spoke when it was called for. Remained silent when you needed to. And, most important..."

She trailed off.

"And most important?"

"Most important, Conner, you let me do my job," she said.

Was that what I did?

"I tell you, Jenny, you were a pleasure to watch. An artist at work."

She gave me a shy grin. As I looked away I saw the grin fade and I saw her glance at Mai. Disappointment. Might have wondered more about that. Didn't.

"You looked to be born to it," Bobbie Lee agreed.

"I don't know about that, youngster," she said.

Bobbie Lee put on what he called his best smile. "Youngster yourself, you've dealt cards a lot. When did you have the time?"

"Not all that much. Not really." She shook her head.

"How then?" I asked.

"Hiram, my husband, may he rest in peace, loved poker. Loved it," Jenny said. "I went with him. I watched. I learned."

"He won at the casinos?" Bobbie Lee marveled, wide-eyed in disbelief.

"Hiram was good, but he didn't trust casinos. He was a rounder."

"A rounder?" I asked.

"Rounders are expert players that go looking for games. Like yours, Conner," Jenny explained. "We'll have to look out for those showing up here."

I nodded. "Watch out for them cheating?"

"Hey, cheats are cheats. Rounders will probably be good for us. Especially if we get two or three coming in for the night." Jenny gave an encouraging wink. "They are exciting to watch. And they'll want long games. If their luck holds. We'll have a good rake."

I took up the cash stack that would be Rose Maceo's cut and put it in the heavy cotton bag we'd kept for that purpose. *United States Bank*, in faded blue ink, marked its original owner. I folded it neat and shoved it in my jacket pocket.

"Now yours," I said to Jenny. "Thirty-five dollars."

Twenty-five went to Bobbie Lee and ten to Joe. Twenty to Mai. They seemed pleased to add it to their separate wads. There would be ten each for the other two of my crew—Dutch Molen and Yuli Ayo.

When they got back. What was left went first to expenses. Liquor for the bar. Some food. The sealed decks of cards Jenny never had enough of. God knew what else. Anything left was mine. That might amount to fifty-eight dollars. Almost felt rich.

By the time I rolled the bills in with my wad, somebody rapped knuckles on the door.

As relaxed as Bobbie Lee appeared, his hand dipped into his jacket, where his pistol tucked into his belt. The door opened and two smiling faces leaned through.

The rest of my crew.

Dutch might have been Bobbie Lee's colossal second cousin. Blond hair thicker than his and wavy. Big-boned, solid-muscle frame almost too tall to make it through the door. A rock of a jaw wrapping a crooked smile of crooked teeth. Pale blue eyes set too close together, with one of them surrounded by puffed, blue bruises. Dutch carried the quiet, even-tempered happiness of a giant, sure in his ability to stomp down anything or anyone that chose to get in his way. Anything except a load of booze that fell from its netting and busted his knee. The cause of a permanent limp.

Yuli Ayo, a dark and fierce-eyed sailor, hailed from somewhere in Eastern Europe. He jumped from the cargo ship whose load fell on Dutch, and pulled him from the Gulf. He literally jumped ship, refusing to return. Instead, he nursed Dutch all the way back to the hospital. The were been inseparable ever since.

Dutch worked hard to teach Yuli English. The language came slow to him.

"Rough night?" I marked Dutch's shiner.

"Nah," Dutch said. "Couple of drunk soldiers pawing the girls over at the Kit Kat. Lucky punch."

Yuli laughed. "Soldier sleeps good now. Sleep 'til Tuesday, betcha."

"Luck didn't have a damn thing to do with it." Dutch shot a glance at his friend.

"Oh, you're such a brute," Jenny teased and gave a fake shudder. Dutch grinned.

"Come over here and get paid," I said, taking up some bills.

"What for you pay me, Mr. Miles?" Yuli asked.

"You're my crew. You get your cut."

"They paid us already," Dutch said.

"That's for the up-and-down. This is your share for the poker." The up-and-down was what we called patrolling the Beach Gang's various casinos and dance clubs. The Gang did its best to look for and handle its own trouble. Kept our marks feeling safe and the coppers out of our hair.

"Oh, yeah, I forgot," Dutch started. "I talked to a couple of brushes. Already got a couple of players coming Friday. Got a couple of other guys looking."

That was good news.

"Where abouts?" I asked.

"A guy down at the Magruder Hotel, and a George down at the train station."

Georges were colored men that helped folks with luggage coming off the Pullman cars. Galveston visitors would ask these men for whatever excitement might be found around town.

"That's good, boys," I said. "Good job."

Both men grinned, happy with the compliment.

"Ha! The only people that did any kind of job tonight was Jenny and me." Mai stood in the kitchen doorway wiping her hands with a bar towel. "Which one of you joys are gonna drive us home?"

I watched Jenny leave, those long legs swaying, as Bobbie Lee walked the two women out to the Studebaker.

THE SEASON

The brushes did us good. Kept marks coming in to play.

Mai kept showing up with her girlish smiles and giggles each night. She convinced me she liked to pour drinks into my marks. She convinced me she didn't miss the income gotten from her chosen trade. Jenny kept being Jenny. Oh, how she charmed as those cards flew back and forth across the table. Our marks fell under her spell, her smile full of welcome and mischief.

The money came in. Steady and sure. The weeks passed. November bled into December.

The first Monday of the month. The only thing listed was a trip down to give the Maceo brothers their cut from the weekend's poker. Back quick after an easy drop off. A nice easy day, so I thought.

A garland of pine and red ribbon hung from the front door. Christmas had come to the house.

Contrary Mary's shiny pickup truck was parked on the street. Organized chaos inside. Dianne and Mary walked around to place Christmas cards everywhere they could find empty space. Jenny and Bobbie Lee decorated a small tree someone mounted on the corner table. Mai stood at the bar stirring up some concoction in a punch bowl. To my surprise, Ol' Dr. Kennedy, Dr. Fix It, helped her.

"No. No. Wait. Wait," Jenny yelled when she caught sight of me. "Turn around. You can't see."

She ran over to a wooden whiskey case full of something or other. Christmas presents, I guessed. She and it disappeared into the back of the house.

"Surprise, Conner." Dianne Starr ran up and wrapped me up in a big hug. I thought more to distract me from Jenny and her crate than anything else.

She was a little thing, and she pressed her head against my chest. I looked over her blond curls to Bobbie Lee. "What's this then?"

"Jenny thought we needed to cheer the place up. You know, for the season and all." he said, shy, like I'd not approve. "You don't mind, right?"

"Conner, come here. Give it a taste," Mai called out. She and Doc Kennedy hovered over the punch bowl.

Bobbie plucked at my sleeve. "Doc wanted to see you. Mary brought him over."

"Let me get my coat off," I said, giving Dianne a last squeeze.

Coat and fedora. The heat in the room was nice after the cloudy cold outside. I could even feel it once I came back from my bedroom.

Bobbie Lee, at his Victrola, stirred up some blues, heavy on the saxophone. I couldn't help making a liquid, swaying shuffle over to Mai. She held out a glass of the red punch. Something sweet and heavy with gin.

I coughed. "Smooth, Mai."

She giggled, covering her cupid bow lips with an open hand. "That's not what I reached for."

"Well, you reached it. Whatever it is."

"Hi, Conner," Doc Kennedy said.

"Hi, Doc. Been a while."

"Has been." He peered closely at the black spot on my lower right eyelid. A piece of metal shrapnel he left there after I was shot at last summer. "That thing bother you any?"

"Don't know it's there 'less I see it in the mirror."

"Good."

"Glad you came by," I said, not meaning it. I never would be glad to see the man, I didn't think.

"Give me a couple of minutes, when you can."

"Sure, Doc. Let me catch up on a few things."

He nodded and took a glass of Mai's liquid fire. I went to Jenny.

She hung more glittering glass ornaments on the tree. Smelled pleasant up close. So did the tree.

"Nice. Electric lights," I marveled. "This'll be my first Christmas tree lighted up."

"A string of eight," Jenny said. "Bought 'em for twelve dollars over at Janssen's."

"Damn, Jenny, that's a chunk of change."

"But they're so pretty. Could have rented them. A buck fifty. Hell, we can keep them for next year," she said. Her eyes got worried. "You don't mind all this, I hope. You said we could."

"I don't mind, Jenny. Kind of surprised you got Dianne and Mary over."

"Ran into them out shopping. Dianne loved the idea. Said you needed something like this. Said her place near drowned in Christmas cards. She volunteered to bring some over."

"Lots of Christmas wishes from her satisfied customers?"

Jenny broke out a big grin. "Lots. And very satisfied. I read a few of them."

Couldn't wait to read them. "Did we get any word from our brushes?"

"I think Dutch and Yuli are out checking now. Lots of folks down for Christmas, I expect."

"Hope so," I said. "You have any idea what Doc's doing here?"

"He didn't say."

The last time I saw Doc Kennedy, he picked out bits of metal from my face and swabbed me with Mercurochrome. Not gently. I was not eager to talk with him.

"You know, Conner." Jenny touched my arm. "You have the only sour face in the room. If you can't put a smile on your lips, let some of Mai's punch do it."

Doc was over there. I shrugged. "Yeah. All right."

"More?" Mai asked. She took my glass without waiting for an answer.

"What 'cha need, Doc?" I took the punch from Mai but kept my eyes on Kennedy.

"A ride back to my office," he said.

Well that screwed up my face. "Good Lord, why?"

"I want to show you something. Back at my office."

"Something I'd like, right?"

"Something you're likely to hate. I'm asking anyway. Reasons. You know."

"Reasons?"

He shrugged a nod. "Reasons. Might be worth your time."

Doc Kennedy held back something. Why?

"Rose suggested it," he added.

Damn. Whatever Rose Maceo, my boss, suggested was no suggestion at all.

"Hey," I said to the room. "I'm taking Doc back."

Got so focused on the man and what he hadn't said that I forgot my flogger. Chilly as hell ride to the Doc's office. A building facing Broadway he shared with a furniture store and a dress shop. I had to look close to see it. A heavy, fancy door with a brass plaque naming him. No big windows like the two stores. The door opened to a walk-up. Doc's suite was upstairs on the left.

Typical waiting room but with a haunted feeling. Several secondhand lounge chairs around the wall. A secondhand, oaken desk for an absent receptionist. A secondhand coffee table holding several well-used magazines.

His office was as expected. Maybe a little less haunted. Big desk matched the one in the front room. Two leather-covered chairs. Tall, heavy bookshelves, crammed with medical books, towered up the wall behind his desk. Beside that were two large file cupboards and a glass-fronted apothecary cabinet that bulged with various concoctions. Under the office windows sat a substantial chaise lounge with brass feet and dark green, fabric cushions.

"Pull that chair up, please," he directed.

I did, then watched as he rifled through one of his desk drawers.

He made a show of it, I thought. Played for drama. Out came a folder. From there, he slapped a large photograph before me.

A woman from chin to the top of her head laying on a dark metal table. A dead woman, face fixed in apparent disapproval. Eyes dark-shadowed, half-opened, pupils dilated. Lips crooked, as if pinched together by someone. Light-colored hair, skewed and lank.

"Christ, Doc. Damn," I snarled. "What's with you and dead people?"

The first time I saw the man, he was leaning over a body. He just looked at me.

"Did the Handmaiden send you over to me?" I asked. The Hand-maiden was Dianne Starr's nickname and it clued folks to how she made her living. "Is this another one of her messes?"

"No. It's not," he said.

"Did Rose?"

It might be just like Rose Maceo to get me stirred into a death.

Doc nodded.

"Why include me?"

"Because of her." He pointed at the picture. I stared at him, stumped. "Let me introduce you to Victoria Yeats. Found dead in her bungalow, as the papers put it. They buried the story on page four."

"So?"

"So, the widow, Mrs. Yeats, was murdered, though the lid's down tight on that. Roughed up, too. Badly. And after that…"

Doc pulled out another picture. I grimaced, steeling myself. Through a doorway, a lounge chair sat in the middle of the room, facing out at the camera.

"…After that, someone watched her die. She was found on the floor just about where the cameraman took his shot."

"Damn, Doc, the coppers probably moved the chair."

"They said not." He reached back into that drawer.

"Oh please. Don't show me more pictures," I begged.

Kennedy relented and sat back with his bemused smile that I began to hate.

"Mrs. Yeats wore a robe when she was found," he said. "A robe, and nothing else. It was opened, and the chair had been moved in front of her. I think, Conner, that someone watched. She was poisoned. Have ideas which ones, but don't know, yet. She took a long time to die."

Christ on a crutch. Horrid thought.

"Did you tell the coppers that?"

Kennedy nodded.

"And?"

"And they didn't give a damn. Simple that she did herself. The simplest is the best downtown."

I let out a filthy curse.

I didn't make any promises to Doc Kennedy. Kept telling myself all the way back to the house that I wouldn't.

My guys were there, draped across the chairs. They stared at me, curious. Dianne had taken all her girls, and Contrary Mary, and left. The Christmas cheer remained and glittered at me.

Their curiosity got left unanswered.

"So the ladies are gone," I said. The methane warmth in the room felt wonderful after the frigid drive back.

"A shame that," Jenny said. "Like all the life fled from the room."

As Mai passed me a drink, I gave Jenny a wink. "These pugs are blind and deaf. You and Mai are the heart and heat of this place."

"God help me against your Paddy blarney. You gonna give this poor girl the sugars." Jenny winked back. Pleased, I think.

Getting the sugars meant becoming diabetic.

I moved over to the space heater, appreciating the smell of scorched bricks and bright-lit pine resin. "Glad to see you all busy getting ready for tonight."

That cleared the chairs. Clatter and shuffle echoed through the house. They all had to appear to be busy. Wafts of Lily of the Valley and sandalwood eased up near my shoulder. My slow, deep breath came without orders from my brain.

"Soir de Paris." Jenny pronounced it Swar-de-Paree. "Like it?"

"I sure do."

"Gift from Contrary Mary."

"You're kidding me."

"Nope. The woman knows her perfumes."

I gave Jenny a toe to head gaze. "Knows her women too, I think."

Jenny flushed to her earlobes.

"So what did Kennedy want?" she asked after her own deep breath.

"To give me a whole new set of nightmares. The bastard," I said, remembering the dead skirt on the slab.

"He brought you other nightmares?"

"The man swims in them. Almost like we swim in marks."

"All right, Conner, the question's begged. Why is he bringing you nightmares?"

I didn't have a chance to reply because the answer headed up my steps.

"Conner?" Dutch called out. "The Boss is outside."

"The Boss?"

"Rose." Dutch, wide-eyed, nodded furiously as he went for the door.

Well, hell. The day just kept on giving.

Rosario "Rose" Maceo reminded me of the small town barber he used to be. Handsome enough. Well fed. Sad eyed. At first glance. On a second look, I saw the eyes behind the puppy droop. Razor-sharp eyes that missed nothing made Judgment Day fall on whoever he looked at. Always vivid to me was the day he found Bobbie Lee and me sweeping sidewalks downtown on the only day that week the two of us weren't hungry. Well, not all that hungry. Midnight that same day I pulled bootlegged whiskey from a speedboat way down on West Beach. Rose Maceo's whiskey. A small town barber in a hundred dollar suit and a thirty dollar Fedora.

I owed Rose Maceo.

I recognized the two men he brought with him. Members of his personal crew. Each bore bulges beneath their left armpits and frowns on their mugs. I didn't know their names and I knew they would not be introduced.

"Good evening, Mr. Maceo." I nodded to him and to his two men. "Something to drink?"

"Evening, Mr. Miles," he said in that rumble that was part Sicilian peasant, part Cajun drawl. "Not for me, t'anks."

"Dutch, their coats. Mai, get something warming to drink," I ordered. Mai was already pouring. The men kept their coats. They took the drinks.

Rose decided to walk around. He grinned at the tree, with its eight glaring bulbs.

"Dat's nice, Miles. Lights on mine at da house. Wife, she likes 'em. The kids."

He turned and grabbed one of the Christmas cards from the mantle. He read it and made a face.

"All these cards came from Dianne Starr," I explained.

"Somebody had a *joyeux* Noël," he said. Sounded like ess-sway-you Noël.

I nodded.

"Let's talk. *Oui*?" Rose asked.

"Let's."

I led him back to the starkly furnished room. Chairs and a couch. Two mismatched floor lamps and a table. An ashtray. A door I could close. Which I did.

We sat. The rising star of the Beach Gang watched me a minute.

"You saw Dr. Kennedy?" Right down to business.

"Yessir," I answered. Rose looked at me until I realized he wanted something more. "Somebody's got something coming."

He nodded. "Yes, *mon cher*, somebody sure does. Do you know this woman?"

"No." I shook my head.

"She's Donny Colleta's fluff. You know Colleta?"

"I know of him."

"Colleta's been with Ollie Quinn since ever. Runs dat Pelican Club up the beach." Some touch of reverence in his voice as he dropped the big boss's name.

"Oh yeah. I've seen it." I remembered the square, red brick thing with the big windows. Dining and dancing up front. Roulette and slots around back.

"Colleta's important folks, Miles. Damn fool, but important."

"Fool?"

"His fluff got herself kilt dead. And dat fool's a married man." Rose gave me a look. "Important married. Wife's da daughter of a honcho in da Norleans mob."

Big time New Orleans gangster. I swallowed hard.

"Means you gotta keep the leather cinched up tight, Miles. Don' go getting you butt in the papers, yeah?"

No more doubts. I hunted a murderer for Rose Maceo. "Close and quiet. Yessir."

Rose nodded back at me and waited. I needed to say something more.

"The Town guys stirring up stuff?" I asked. The Town Gang were our rivals.

"Nah. Don't think so. That sit down we had back in summer got things worked out. But, if you run into any of 'em, you get to me, *bientôt*."

Bientôt—pronto, as soon as… I nodded agreement. "How about enemies? Does he have any?"

Rose laughed starting deep in his chest. Deep rumble. Infectious.

"Runs a casino. What you think?"

"Well, maybe she had enemies herself."

"Like Colleta's wife?" Rose asked.

"Maybe. Do you know anything about this Victoria woman?"

Eyebrows arched up as Rose looked away from me. He pursed his lips.

"I'm a married man, *cher*," he said. "A family man. I take seriously my family. Donny Colleta, he takes his family seriously Saturday night. Sunday night. Friday night, he does not. I see the fluff some Fridays. At some of my places. Charm the scales off a cobra. Charmed Colleta shu 'nuff…"

Rose looked off, wistful. Wistful. He snapped back.

"I know this. Da woman kept Donny smilin.' Before her, this swamp rat never knew that man to show a fang 'less he got to bitin' somebody, I guarantee." Rose drawled out gair-uun-tee.

To me that was about the best recommendation a piece of fluff could get.

"She cut up? Pass herself around? Be an embarrassment? Seen playing around with some other girls?"

Rose went all flint-eyed. "Hope you be rumbling out loud to yourself, Miles."

After a hard swallow into a cold belly, I remembered who I talked to. The man, by his nature would not know, or want to know, or would admit he knew these things about the woman. "Yessir. Sorry. Talking to myself. Swear."

He reached into his jacket pocket and fished out a heavy, old-style skeleton key that had some kind of tag tied to it with a string.

"This is the key to the woman's house. Address, too. We kept the coppers tamped down on this thing. Didn't let 'em tear da place up. You go down there. See what you can find out."

He handed over the key.

A warning sprung up in me. "Mr. Maceo, does Mr. Colleta know about this? I don't want to be stepping on toes. Especially important toes."

Rose's softer smile turned him back into that small town barber. "Colleta talked to Ollie Quinn. Quinn talked to me. Me, *cher*, I talk to you."

"So he knows I'm looking into it."

"He knows someone is."

I guessed that'd have to do.

Mr. Maceo looked quickly around the stark room, then chinned toward the closed door.

"Out there, *cher*. You done pretty good. Like it? Makin' money."

Didn't think that last was a question. Because Mr. Maceo counted his cut. He knew well enough how much money I made.

"Yessir. Thank you."

"Colleta is important people. Dis—this tang, it's gotta be took care of," Rose started. "But I tell you this…"

Again, he chinned toward the front of the house.

"What you got there, out there is more important. Don't think I don't know it. You 'member that too, *cher*."

"I will, Mr. Maceo."

"Good, that. You take care of this for us. Somebody's gotta pay."

"Yessir, Mr. Maceo.

For us, he said. Take care of it for us. Marching orders coming down from the Throne of Heaven. From Ollie Quinn himself. I felt a cold sweat coming on. Kind of glad to have the brace of chill wind when I escorted Rose and his men out of the door.

The marks were due soon. The game counted most.

A SHOTGUN HOUSE

Spatters of rain, wind-driven, insulted me as I got out of the Studebaker. A tug down on my fedora's brim, another to gather my overcoat tighter, and I took the flagstones toward Victoria Yeats' front steps.

A shotgun house not out of place in the run down and declining neighborhood. Called a shotgun house because if a man let off both barrels of buckshot into the front door, the scatter of lead traveled clear down a central hall and straight out the back door. Had them back home in East Texas, but it jarred me because Victoria Yeats' sat high on red brick pilings. Required on all Island housing since the 1900 Hurricane that wiped most of the town off the map. In the hope that the pilings raised the houses above any future storm surge. Like most of the houses along the street, it needed new paint. Not all that bad, for enough naked wood showed on the steps to prevent them being slippery.

I fished out the heavy key and pulled open the tattered screen door. Before the key found the keyhole, Victoria's front door flung itself open. Near scared the pee out of me.

"So, you coppers don't knock anymore?" said the most classically beautiful face I had ever clapped orbs on.

Wide green eyes, bold nose, cupid-bow lips, face framed in a glow of brunette waves of hair. Kept long, not bobbed. White, long-cut cardigan over white slacks. Sock-footed. No jewelry.

Cleared my throat and breathed again before I could talk.

"I'm not the police."

She noticed the breath and tried to stop the corners of her mouth from turning up.

"Then what are you doing with the key to this house?"

"What are you doing already in this house?" Don't know where exactly that came from, but I was glad it came. Saint Michael's very toenails, that girl was good to look at.

"You first." She glared.

I considered a moment. Just how much could I tell?

"No. You first. Why are you in Miss Yeats' house?"

"It's Mrs. Yeats. She is—was—my Aunt. I actually belong here. Now you?"

More considering. What did this skirt know about her Aunt?

"Do you know Mr. Colleta?"

"Donny? Sure, I know him. Is that who you got the key from? Damn. One of his gangsters. My day just keeps getting better."

Gangster or gambler, or bootlegger? Had to wonder just what I was as I stood in front of this woman. Girl, really. A quick picture of my poker game flashed in my mind. I didn't think I was sure yet. There might not be much difference.

"I asked you a question," she went on.

"The name's Miles. Conner Miles. Mr. Colleta asked me to come. To look things over." A lie but only part of a lie.

"You a shamus? You're young for a shamus."

"No. I'm a gambler." It looked like I'd decided after all. Surprised at that.

"That's gotta be some kind of a jive gangster. Donny rolling dice over my Aunt's body?"

I made a look around and tried to hunker deeper into my coat. Made a point to. Looked back at the skirt.

"Well, whatever you are, you don't look all that dangerous. Come on." She stepped back to open the door.

Warm air. Thank goodness.

"I'd thank you, if I knew your name."

Eyes that could melt paint looked at me. "Susanna, but call me Windy. It's Windy not Wendy. Not Peter Pan's bit of calico. I got the name because I yapped a lot in grade school."

"Thank you, Windy," I said, taking off my fedora. Like my mama taught me.

The gratitude seemed to challenge her for some reason. The sudden fire in her eyes made her look less like a church statue. "I'd give even money, Gambler, that folks have names for you, too."

"Mick, Paddy, Bogtrotter. I got ya' beat." I smiled my best smile.

Windy chuckled. A deep rich chuckle. "You do for sure."

A touch of an edge to Windy. Didn't dislike it. But I finally took my eyes off of her and got a surprise. Victoria's shabby shotgun house on the outside was an Art Deco marvel on the inside. Top drawer elegance, at least in the front room.

"Like it?" she asked.

"Impressive."

"It's Mr. Miles, right?" she asked. I nodded. "So is that all the look over you need to do?"

"You know it's not." I fought a war inside about just how much of a lid could I keep on things and still get past Windy Wright.

"Spill it, gambler. Why are you here?"

"I'm to find who got to your Aunt. And this is where I'm starting."

Windy stirred up a pure, angel, virgin glow that I later learned to be Romantic Era art. Caused my Irish heart to roll right over. "The papers are saying it might be a suicide."

"You know it's not," I repeated. "My people want the deck cleared. We want who did this. Donny wants who did this."

She got thoughtful. I let her think.

"That's why the law's not climbing all over the place then."

I nodded.

"I know who Donny is. I know what he's like. Why isn't he doing this himself?" she probed.

"Two reasons." Guesses really but I thought them close to the truth. "He sits high on the pole for one."

"Hands keep clean."

"Yes."

"And two?"

"Two is that there are people who'd love to chop him down off that pole. Can't get him tangled up in something like this."

"So you get to take the blame."

Hmm, hadn't really considered that angle. "I'll try to avoid that if I can."

"Okay, Gambler, want to rummage through Victoria's undies?"

I grimaced. "Not that. I want to see things that let me get to know her some. What she did? Who her pals were? What was her life like? Things like that."

"Who her enemies were?" Windy Wright gestured across the room. "Have your look."

So I did. Art Deco—glitzy and ritzy, and glittery. Gold, silver, black, red. Stark, pure colors. Metallic fixtures. Ethereal posters on the wall. Marbled tables.

"Do you like it?"

I looked around the room, awed. "Beyond anything I've seen before."

"I mean the picture." She pointed to a poster prominently placed over the fireplace.

Posters like this decorated things all over New Orleans. A nymph or fairy seated on a stone bench under a tree whose flowers were falling in an invisible breeze. The nymph, a young girl, wore a filmy, gauzy nightshirt that only barely hid her small breasts. Some birds I'd never seen in my Texas forests seemed to flit. All in pastels and everything appeared almost transparent.

"Very nice," I said.

"Look closer," she ordered. I did. "Look higher."

I checked out the upper frame.

"No. Are all gangsters so thick?" she pouted. "Look at the face. The face."

A child's face filled with mischief and curiosity. Windy's face.

"You were a baby."

"Not that young. The painter made me look younger. Strange man. But I only sat for him about two years ago. Do you like it?"

"It's wonderful."

"And it's mine, now. I'll be glad to get it. Finally."

Later I learned the word avarice. Avarice shone bright in her eyes.

"Yours?"

"Victoria had it done. She liked it, so she kept it. It's mine now."

One more sweep of the room followed by a sigh. I needed to shift the subject. "Jesus! Mr. Colleta really helped her out."

"Well, Jesus and I guess so. But Victoria was pretty good at helping out herself," she retorted. Her eyes followed mine, looked across the room but came back to mine. I saw some challenge in them.

"Didn't mean anything by it. Sorry."

"You say sorry a lot, Gambler," she said. "So, what did you learn?"

"That Victoria Yeats was one modern type of skirt."

"Skirt, huh. Is that what they call us in your circles?"

"I'm..." Started to say, I'm sorry. Put fingers across my lips instead.

Windy's laugh was a deep, low chortle. I liked it.

"Anything in here special to her, that you know about?"

"My Aunt liked all this. Specially. She was proud of what she had."

"But nothing precious? Nothing pulling at her heart strings?"

She scrunched up that pretty face as she gave the room another once over.

"I don't know. I don't think so, except for my painting. Is that the kind of thing you're looking for?"

Her painting now.

"I don't know what exactly. Something else."

Windy considered me for a moment. Disconcerting having one so good to look at looking at me so frankly.

"Come on then. I'm here picking up some stuff mother wanted."

She swooped from the room. I hadn't seen someone swoop before. Not like Windy. What a walk in those pale, clingy slacks. I followed, hardly aware of putting one foot in front of the other. Hardly aware of dining room, or kitchen, or bath.

Windy turned left into an Oriental-themed bedroom. More reds, golds, and blacks framing all the colors I ever knew. Black-lacquered Armoire and vanity. A dressing screen showing scenes of Chinese ladies picnicking in exotic mountains. A dark wood, four-poster bed. In contrast, some milk crates, beat up and crowded with a lot of this and that.

"Things my mother wanted," Windy gestured to the crates. She knelt next to them, pulling her feet beneath her, Comanche style. That angelic smile invited me to sit with her.

I did just that.

"What's all here?" I asked, fingering a hand-size, framed picture. Victoria posed with a dark-haired, striking man standing next to her in a garden. A wedding picture, though the man wore an army uniform. Not Donny Colleta. "She's married?"

Windy's smile went sad. "She was."

"Divorced? Died in the war?"

"No, no. He came back from Belgium. Came back half deaf. Artilleryman, but he lived through it. Flu got him in '18."

Ouch. I'd lost relatives and friends from that huge epidemic.

"Sorry."

Windy shrugged those sculpted shoulders. "He was nice enough. But, her husband, not mine."

"I'm still sorry."

"Past hope, past cure, past help." She stared down at the floor.

"What?"

"Shakespeare. I quote him a lot. One of the reasons they call me Windy."

I actually knew of Shakespeare. Hadn't read him yet, but I knew of him. Still, I began to feel that quote myself.

The next thing I pulled from her crate was a dark, wooden box the size of two fists pressed together.

"Yes. My grandmother's music box." She took it from my hand and cranked the key. "Victoria got this when Granny passed. I envied her. So did my mother. She'll like having it."

Windy and her mother had special feelings for many of Victoria's things. She listened to the tolling chimes, a dreamy look in her eye.

"How was her marriage? Victoria's?" I wondered how the woman went from wife to gangster's mistress in those few years.

"All right, as far as I know. Mostly, I guess." She seemed hesitant.

"Mostly?"

"I remember them over for Christmas just after he got back. He really couldn't hear much. Victoria got, what? Got kind of testy with him. His not picking up things she said to him.

"She had a bit of a temper, then?"

Windy picked a figurine from the crate. Couldn't really see what it was. "Shakespeare said, 'Do you know I am a woman? When I think, I must speak.' My Aunt had a mouth. And she wasn't slow at speaking her mind."

"She that way around Mr. Colleta?"

"You know, Gambler, I'm not so far above being a little girl. I wasn't around the two of them all that much…"

"But?"

"But, yeah," Windy said. "What she thought, she spoke."

"How did Colleta take that?"

"As far as I know?" she quizzed.

"Yes. As far as you know."

She laughed her magical laugh. Low and deep. "It seemed to amuse him. I don't think much rattles the man."

I promised myself I'd give that some thought later.

"Do you have any idea what Victoria was doing right before…?"

"Before she died, you mean?"

I nodded.

"No idea at all."

"Damn." It was a mutter.

"Language, Gambler. The presence of what I hope is a lady."

Lady enough, I thought, looking at her. She noticed.

"So, you got me ranked?"

"I'm sorry?"

"You're looking at me like you're doing some comparative shopping. How do I rank?"

I laughed and gave her an honest answer. "Top of the list, Windy."

Her shy smile turned her back into a young girl.

"La, I'll go on past that," she said. But I thought she was pleased. "I might know someone. Who might know what she was doing. Before."

"Get me a meeting. Can you?"

"I can try. Call me in a couple of days."

Exciting for a number of reasons. "What's your number?"

Mischief spread all over her, face and body. "I'm in the book. Or, my parents are. I live there."

Would have been all to the good had I not been so flummoxed that I forgot to ask their names.

Windy ushered me out. I thanked her. I probably needed the ushering. She closed the door and I stared at it for too long a moment. Jesus, that girl was nice to look at. I was blind to anything else walking to the Studebaker. Should not have been.

Rounding the car's grill, I stepped right into an uncoiling snake in the form of a Fedora, an overcoat, and the four clicks of a Colt revolver being cocked.

Stuck up close to my nose, that damned pistol looked like a cannon.

"Who the hell are you?" came a gravelly snarl.

I did a quick check, to feel if I'd wet my pants, then went from scared to angry.

"The goddamned Fuller Brush man. Who the hell are you?"

"I done killed two Fuller Brush men, fool. Give me the straight dope or you'll be floatin' in the Bay before dark. What 'cha doing here?"

"Donny Colleta sent me over." Well, that was only part of a lie.

"Now what the hell would Mr. Coletta want a dumb kid like you to come nosing around this place?"

"Ask him. It's not your business."

"It is my business. I'm watching the place for him. So, quit the stall."

"If he didn't tell you, I'm not." I looked back down at that hand cannon. "Sorry."

"Are you just wantin' me to put a hole in you?"

Damn. "Mister, know that I'm more afraid of Ollie Quinn than I am of that pistol."

Never hurt to drop a name. I felt the heavy thrum of blood pulsing up my neck. That bastard's eyes showed he'd shoot me down as sure as sunset.

Those eyes shifted to something over my shoulder. A car engine rumbled, getting closer.

My tormentor eased his gat into his coat pocket. "Keep real still, Fuller Brush man."

Be sure I did. That blessed car pulled right up in front of mine. Its engine popped a couple of times. I flinched at each pop. Its emergency break ripped tight. I ventured to look over my shoulder—and lived.

A cocky-looking kid got out. Yellow and red college sweater. Knickerbockers. Yellow and red matching socks. Brown and white oxford shoes.

"Hubba, hubba, oldsters," the kid said and made long strides up to Victoria's house.

I shared an eye roll with the thug.

"Quick, fool, give me a name. I gotta tell it to Mr. Colleta," he growled.

"Miles. The name is Miles."

My hands, stinging cold, slipped into my coat. My thug watched closely before he turned to go to a Model T parked a block down.

I just watched, not trusting my knees to move me quite yet. Victoria's door opened and Windy came out to tuck a gloved hand under the kid's arm. He walked her down to his car.

"Well, Gambler," she said. "You have interesting friends."

"Don't I ever," I said.

"You all right?"

"Peachy. Cold though."

"Let me hear from you," she said, earning a raised eyebrow from her friend with the knickerbockers.

I nodded. The two of them puttered off down the street. They turned heading toward Broadway.

My Studebaker took the turn toward Seawall. Last I saw, the thug's Model T sat right where it was.

TELEPHONES

I never made it to Seawall. Hadn't settled the storm in my gut from visions of Windy and of staring down the barrel of a revolver. I let the sun set behind me and ate a blue plate supper over on Mechanic Street.

Dutch opened the door for me just before eight.

"Good to see you, boss." He smiled.

Boss? A boss and a gambler. I made the point to remind myself of that.

The place looked ready to go. I had good help. Smiling Mai shoved a big dose of Irish in my hand and took my flogger and Fedora.

"Making Sidecars for the marks tonight," she said, sidling toward the coat rack.

"What's that?" I asked.

"Mostly Bourbon and triple-sec."

"We have Bourbon?"

"We sure do." Joe popped out of his chair. "Yuli and Dutch helped down at the tracks. Got lots of good stuff. Including a couple of crates straight from Canada."

He walked up to me fishing a wad from his pants. Deft fingers peeled six double saw bucks from its center.

"Your cut, to date." Joe handed the bills over.

One hundred twenty dollars in six pieces of government green paper.

"Nice. Dutch, Yuli, thanks." I looked around. "Where is Yuli?"

"He's out unloading some Rye he got. Down by Fort Crockett somewhere."

"Y'all got Rye?" I asked Dutch.

He nodded. "The Bourbon, some Rye, and a bunch of different kinds of Canadian blends."

"Good job, boys. You're making me proud."

Joe and Dutch grinned, truly pleased. That surprised me. It was an easy enough thing to say.

Jenny waited for me in her place at the poker table. I gave her the liquor cut. She would put it with the house take, where it would be divided between ours and Maceo's cut.

"So?" Jenny sing-songed and looked at me with her old-soul, green eyes.

"Sooo, what?"

"How was your day? What did you do with your time?"

Again the questions inside me. What to tell? How much to tell?

"Mr. Maceo wants me to look into some things. I looked into some things."

Jenny began fiddling with the chip tray, waiting.

"Ever heard of Victoria Yeats or Susanna Wright?" I asked.

Her brows raised. "Susanna? You mean Windy Wright?"

I nodded.

"Well, I know her parents. Her mamma teaches all the dancing over at the Opera House. Her father has an acting school down-town."

"How about Victoria Yeats?"

Jenny shook her head. "No."

"She's Mrs. Wright's sister."

"Don't know her," she said.

"She's dead. Murdered most likely."

"That's balled up, Conner."

"Eggs well scrambled, more like."

"Anything you can share?" she asked. I saw she tried hard to look helpful and not curious.

"Not much," I answered. "Got to call her, Windy, in a couple of days."

Bobbie Lee showed up, causing Jenny and I to go silent.

"Gee, quiet all of a sudden. Y'all must be talkin' about me," He said as he sat down on my left.

"Actually we were talking about telephones."

"Yeah. We don't have one," Bobbie Lee said.

"You should get one. Amazing things, telephones. Can't live my life without one," Jenny said.

"Nah. They list your name and number in the papers when you get one." I shook my head. "Not sure I want that."

"So put your place name. Good advertising." Bobbie Lee countered.

"Not sure I want to do that either. Don't want that attention. Anyway, the place doesn't have a name," I said.

"Sure it does. I always tell folks I go over to Connie's house when I head this way,"

"Not sure, still," I said.

"Play with it. Make a pun out of it. Like Connie Place," Jenny put in.

"Maybe Connie House. Or, Connie Houseman," Bobbie Lee offered.

"They allow that?" I asked.

"Don't think anyone checks that close." Bobbie Lee may have had information I didn't know.

"I'll need it in two days," I said, still not sure I even wanted one.

"Copacetic. Joe's the man can get it done. Hey Joe!" Bobbie Lee sang out.

Joe raised a hand and nodded. He'd listened. He, I figured, must have known people who knew people.

"That rattle trap from the Hotel is pulling up." Dutch rose from his seat to go to the door.

"Some players for you," Jenny said.

Joe was good for it. In two days I had a telephone I didn't know how to use and my place had a name I didn't like. *Connie Place.*

The day after that, I went out.

The China Clipper promised exotic cuisine. I hoped it offered warmth. The place occupied space on the ground floor of an office building a block off the Strand. Town Gang territory but I went anyway.

A gale of high-pitched laughter seeped through the glass. Windy's promise. A skirt that knew Victoria Yeats.

I don't think I was as scared of Colleta's torpedo and his hand cannon in front of Victoria's house as I was of facing two curious women.

"Just you, sir?" The smooth looking maître d' asked. He took my fedora and my flogger and hung them on a rack.

"I'm joining a party, thank you." More squeals of laughter. I rolled my eyes. "That's them now, I think."

"Oh yes. They said they expected someone." He made a sardonic grin. "Good luck to you, sir."

Needed, I suspected. The shrill laughter fell into a chill silence as I neared the table. Windy graced me with a smile that was a beatitude all on its own. The other woman appraised me as if I was a milk cow at the auction.

"This is Conner," Windy said. "Conner, this is Deirdre."

The woman made a face and an eye roll. "Real people call me Drew."

I took her offered hand and sat across from her.

"So you're Windy's trouble boy," Drew continued.

"Sorry. I don't know what that is," I said.

"Trouble boy. A gangster," she told me. "What do you call them?"

"I usually call them sir."

That caused a laugh, as I'd hoped it would.

"Conner's no gangster. He's a gambler. Just ask him," Windy said. She gave our waiter a nod. Apparently the signal to bring me something to drink.

"Some title. Gambler," Drew said. "What's the life like for a gambler?"

"Nope," I said with a smile. "Didn't come here to talk about me. Came to talk about Victoria."

They went serious.

"Windy said you didn't think she did herself in," Drew said.

"Do you? Either of you?" I asked.

"Neither of us, Conner," Windy said.

"Who'd want to hurt her?" I asked and got blank stares. "Think about it. Maybe Victoria hurt somebody. Somebody that might have a beef with her."

"Oh, I know. How about that mustard plaster that follows her around," Windy said, all wide-eyed.

Drew shuddered. "God, I remember him. What a heebie-jeebie."

"Yeah." Windy turned to me. "He's a dew dropper. Doesn't work. Sleeps all day. He used to follow her around doing the lost puppy act."

"Victoria gave him the icy mitt. More than once. We saw him recently. Couple of weeks back. Still, a bother," Drew added.

"A fellow scorned—if I can get some poetic license on an old phrase," Windy said.

"Dearie, you license poetic all over the place," Drew teased.

I had to ask her. "Was she doing that for all that laughing when I came in?"

"No, Gambler, I laugh so that I do not weep..."

"Anyway, Victoria would not want that. She just would not want anyone all teary-eyed. Anytime," Windy added.

Good for Victoria, I thought. "Where can I find this—what did you call him—this dew dropper?"

"Berries. Easy. He lives around behind Victoria. And a couple of houses down. Has a big garden he's always in. Victoria catches him watching her over his fence now and then."

Definitely on my list.

"Anybody else you can think of?"

Drew furrowed her brow. She was a striking woman. Strong, chiseled bone structure. Those brows required plucking, and she'd done a good job of it. The two of them would have marched through anywhere like Sherman's troops through Georgia.

"You know, there was that cake eater. That sailor, Poul," she said. "He got the bum's rush from Victoria, and he didn't seem to like it much."

"Sailor, I know. What's a cake eater?"

"A cake eater is a guy that shows up at all the dances. Tries to give all the flappers a twirl," Windy said. "But he was not just a sailor. He was an officer. Merchant marine."

"He was a real swan on the dance floor. And, Jesus, was he smooth. To look at and to listen to. Dreamy," Drew added.

"Okay," I marveled. "Why did she turn him down?"

"Let me tell you, Conner, Victoria lived with her eyes wide open," Drew said. "We could both see he was giving his knee…"

"I don't know what that means." Damn, I needed to get out more.

"Means he liked to get in close when he danced with a girl." Windy rolled her eyes.

"Felt like a buffed shoe when I left the floor." Drew gave a rueful smile.

I liked that picture. "And he didn't like it when he—what did you call it—when he got the cold mitt."

"The icy mitt," Drew corrected me. "We got the feeling he took it real personal."

"Merchant Marine? Not Navy?"

"Not Navy. Not coast guard. In fact, not American." Drew shook her head. "Not with that dreamy, sing-song he had."

"German, maybe?" I asked, counting the ships heading out to sea with that guy on board.

"No. Not a harsh enough accent," Drew said. "He sure cut his way through the field of skirts in this town with that voice—and with that blond hair."

"A lion among ladies is a most dreadful thing." Windy quoted without looking at either Drew or me.

"You know him, too?" I asked her.

She nodded. "He's a cake eater, true to his cause. And, like she said, too dreamy to miss."

I gave her the cut-eye then turned back to Drew. "Anyone else you can think of?"

Another furrowed brow, but a longer pause. At the end, Drew drew a joker. Nothing.

"You both are forgetting the obvious. Or maybe you just want to." Windy looked right at me.

"What's so obvious?"

"Victoria's lover himself. Donny Coletta. Or, his wife, yes?"

But for Jenny and Mai, the place sat empty. The space heater hissed and glowed. The Christmas stuff glittered. The couch and chairs waited. I pulled my pocket watch.

"Still early, huh?" I asked.

"That's the hope," Jenny shrugged. She looked enticing in a bronzy satin dress, long-sleeved, with black trim at cuff, collar, and down the front. One of her onyx and gold necklaces acted as a headband. I recognized it and knew she would call it a brain binder. A long string of pearls draped from her throat.

"Marks on the way?"

Mai spoke. "That's the word. Bobbie Lee told me we're supposed to have some coming from the Galvez."

She downright dazzled in a sleeveless, short-hemmed, black dress, glittering with black beads inset. A black lace over-dress, long enough to extend below the knees, covered all. Sparkling, paste diamonds made up her headband.

The marks would have a hard time minding their cards.

"Joe promised one or two in from the train station," Jenny said. "At least after they got hotel rooms."

"Where is everybody?" I asked.

"Bobbie Lee's off shopping," Mai beamed. "For me."

More soberly, Jenny related that the crew went down the beach where the Maceos had some liquor warehoused. Sure as the sun comes up on a Tuesday, they'd get some on their own dime and sell it at a couple of places first.

I went to the bar and poured a generous glass of Scotch. In keeping with dinner at the China Clipper. Took it over to sit with Jenny.

She watched my silent sips.

"Well?"

"Well what?"

"How did your dinner date go?" she pushed, as Mai clattered around, pretending she did not listen.

"Date?" I asked. "Is that what I did?"

"Maybe not, but that girl might have thought it was."

Did Windy? Damn. Not my intention. "It wasn't supposed to be."

"Was anything a help to you?"

"I don't know. Maybe." I took a sip. The Scotch started to warm my insides. "Found out that Yeats had people who might wish her harm."

"I guess that can be a good thing." Jenny made a face.

"Maybe. They called one a dew dropper and another a cake eater. Part of her trail of broken hearts, I guess. Anyway, neither liked rejection."

"You know, having Donny Coletta as a beau might make people think twice about messing with her."

"I don't know, Jenny," Mai said. "Men sometimes don't think things through when they're sniffing at a skirt."

"True enough, if I think on it." Jenny looked at me like I'd be doing the same thing, given the chance.

"Me? No, I'd think long and hard." I shook my head.

Jenny and Mai exchanged one of those womanly glances I'd been getting way too much of that day.

"You going to go find those men?" Jenny asked.

"I'm gonna try. Windy thinks she knows where one of them lives. The other I'll have to hunt down."

Jenny picked up a deck of cards. She shuffled them, looking at me. "Which one?"

"The cake eater. He's foreign, and maybe a sailor."

"Jesus, Conner, he could be on his way to Havana or somewhere by now," Mai said.

"He might."

"Time and tide and weather, Conner," Jenny said. "No real reason he's sailed, however."

"True. But I have no idea how to hunt him down if he's still on the Island."

Jenny chuckled. "Simple. Cake eaters don't just graze on the nosh. Cake eaters are there to dance."

"Dance clubs need looking into, then. Plenty enough of them," I said, mostly to myself.

"I don't know, Conner," Jenny said. "I have a hard time seeing Victoria haunting dance clubs. Nor will the kind of cake eater you're looking for."

"I agree," Mai put in. "Why shovel out a pocket of change with all the free dances around? Especially around Christmas."

"And most of them'll be listed in the rags." Jenny bobbed her head.

"There's even a better source, if you've got the sand for it," Mai said.

Huh, I figured I had guts enough for most things.

"I might could handle it. What dangerous place'll find me cake eaters at dances?"

"Windy Wright, of course." Jenny rocked her head and opened her palms like anybody but a pure fool should know.

Pure fool me. And Jenny again recognized the tell on my mug.

She laughed. "Got you shook up, does she, Paddy?"

I puffed out a breath and looked away from her.

"My God, Jenny, he's speechless." Mai's turn to laugh.

"She's a… She's not a…" I tried. "She's not a kind of skirt I'm used to, is all."

"Not one of Dianne's whores? Not your gun moll type?" Mai asked. "Not a bush baby?"

"No, she's not any kind of yokel or anything. And it's not that."

Jenny leaned over the table, propped on her elbows. "What it is, Mai, is that the girl is right easy on the eyes. A real heart breaker. And our idiot Paddy is struck dumb by a pretty face. Dumb."

She was right. I didn't—wouldn't—admit it. But when I looked at Windy...

"Dammit. Go ahead. Roust me some more."

Jenny threw up surrender hands.

"Peace, Paddy," she said. "Seems to me I remember that girl had a fair share of piss and vinegar, and kitten hiss."

Didn't think I saw that. "So?"

"So, Windy might find it exciting to help hunt down her aunt's killer."

Mai laughed her tiny laugh. "I'm thinking he'd find it easier than asking the poor thing out on a date."

It was, as it turned out.

"How are we going to do it?"

That's how Windy greeted me three days later, at dead Victoria's front door.

For once the bitter cold day shone sunny. The rags promised frost overnight. Rare enough thing on Galveston Island. I shuddered. Not so subtle a hint at Windy.

Windy shook her head. An apology? She reached to place a hand on my arm. "Come in. Come in. I'm sorry. Wasn't thinking."

"Excited, are we?" I stepped into the hot glow of two space heaters.

She giggled and offered me a bright smile. "I guess I am. Now, answer my question? How are we going to do it?"

My return smile wasn't bright.

"Today, what we're gonna do is, what my boss would call have a sit down."

"We're sitting?"

"A sit down," I answered. "Windy, somebody's not gonna be real happy to see us, soon as we know who did this to your aunt."

"I thought it might be dangerous. I'm not afraid, Conner." The sudden fire in her eyes matched the blue flame in the heaters. Her lower lip pouted defiance.

"I still want the sit down. I want you straight on some things." I stepped in out of the cold. That impressive, near pornographic painting of Windy didn't sit in its place on the mantle. "What happened to it?"

"Oh, yes. I took it to the house, hoping my father can get it hung somewhere at The Grand," she said through smiling eyes.

Windy meant The Grand Opera House. An ornate, red brick edifice downtown. I'd seen the carved, white arch over its front door but had never been in it.

"Grab a place," I said and sat on the couch.

"You get straight on some things, gangster. I don't let men give me a bunch of commands." Her arms crossed. She was ready for a fight.

"Let me sum it up then." I raised an opened hand. "Don't forget to duck."

Took a minute for her to truly get what I said. She sobered a bit, I thought.

"Jesus, Conner, you don't think people might be shooting?"

I shrugged. "Don't know. Maybe."

Windy stared off into air for a bit. Some fear on her face, I hoped. She may have need of it.

She shook it off with a shudder. A weak smile came to her church statue face.

"My mother groaned. My father wept. Into the dangerous world I leapt."

"Shakespeare?"

"Blake," she told me. "Still though, I think I need to hear what you wanted to tell me."

Good. I told her what little I knew about staying alive and standing in front of angry and desperate people.

"Holy mother, Conner, you really think there'll be trouble?" Eyes wide and round.

"So far in my life, the more trouble I got ready for, the less of it I had."

Windy looked me deep in the eyes. I felt the blood thump in my neck for that. I sensed that she plumbed me for the truth in what I told her. For sure that girl was something to look at. With some effort, I managed to hold that gaze. What I said, I meant.

"You don't get scared?"

"Of course, I do. Knees shake so much they hardly hold me up."

"Do you run?"

"Sometimes that's the right thing to do. Sometimes there is no running," I bit my lower lip. "A person makes a choice to be where he ends up. Or where he stands. Making that choice means you just got to take what you got coming."

If those magic eyes could've gotten wider, they would have.

"Most of the time what scares me never happens," I continued.

"Most of the time?"

"I'm still here. Kind of surprises me, but I am."

She smiled. Maybe she made a decision. "Aren't you the Knight Errant."

"Who said that?"

"Windy Wright did." Resolve came onto her face. "I'm still here, too. What are we to do?"

"You told me that you know that sailor, yes?"

"In passing. I mean, he's not stepping into my berry patch or anything."

The thug that I am took those words down six or eight different trails.

"He doesn't do what?"

Windy shook an accusing finger at me. "Naughty boy. I mean he doesn't show me any attention. Not like he did to Victoria."

"Just her?"

"Others, too. It seemed like he grazed all around. A woman would have to be a real dumb cuff not to see him sniff around. He had a type and I wasn't it."

I thought that disappointed her. To my way of thinking, a skirt wouldn't mind being ignored by that kind of man. Even a good-looking, foreign man with a uniform.

"I need to bump into this sailor, if I can. Get an eye on him."

"How?"

"Get me into some of those dances. Put a finger on him for me."

Windy made a face and chuckled. "Why, Gambler, watch out. A girl might take that as being asked out on a date."

"A girl might." I smiled. "But that girl better know that I don't dance. And she might want to know she shouldn't try to make me. Not unless she wants to spend a week limping around."

"A real corn shredder, huh?"

Took me a second, but I learned a new term.

"Did shred a few corns in my misspent youth, I guess."

"So, are you at least asking me to help you find Victoria's killer?"

What I really asked was for Windy to help me find that sailor, but I found myself reluctant to dampen her enthusiasm. So, she got a shrug of a nod.

She broke into a broad smile. And, brother, did that girl know how to smile.

"Come on," she gestured. "You want to see that dew dropper's house?"

The not-working, sleeping-all-day, fool seemed to show up at Victoria's elbow way too often. All sad-eyes and sighs, no matter how she put him off. I didn't want to go out in the cold, however.

Windy saw that on my face.

"No. Come on. You can see his house from the back porch. Only takes a second," she encouraged. Even grabbed my arm to half drag me towards the back of the house.

The tight-packed back yards of Victoria's neighborhood missed two things. Tree leaves and laundry on the clothes lines. Didn't miss the wind that came from the Bay. It bit and flattened smoke from the chimneys. Some back yards had white picket fences, some brown. Some had winter-worn hedges. The rest—kind of like open range.

Like Victoria's, most of the whitewashed houses had been ill treated by the Island's salt wind, drab and stained.

"That's the house there." Windy pointed down right.

She laid witchy green eyes on me and saw only puzzle. Lots of houses down that way.

"That one," she pointed again. "Four down. The one with the brown fence."

A second later her arm shot up to point.

"Oh look! It's him. It's the dew dropper!"

I did spot the fence. And, because we stood on the raised back porch, I saw the bowed head puttering around. Then, out of nowhere…

"Hello! Hello!" Windy's theater trained alto echoed across the world.

She yelled and waved her arms.

Had people happened close, they might have heard my cringe and grimace.

"What are you doing" I hissed. She ignored me.

That wave and that huge voice again. "Hello! Here!"

"Stop," I begged.

"Come on. I'm helping." She continued waving both arms.

The fool, confused at first, searched over his fence, finally spotting Windy's flailing arms. I could almost make out his eyes, wide and poking over the top of his weather-stained, wooden fence.

"Wait! Wait there! We'll come to your house!" Windy's opera continued.

"Windy?" I growled.

"What? You wanted my help. Here's a guy that might have hurt Victoria. So, let's go talk to him."

I only thought she'd struck me speechless before. I'd hoped to make time to plan a bit. Felt like being caught flat-footed with a punch to the gut.

"Come on." Windy turned to strut that woman's march back into the house.

Where do women learn that walk? Do their mamas teach it with the second steps out of the cradle? Of course, I followed like my own kind of fool.

The two of us hunched into our coats and bowed against the knifing, cold breeze. My fractured brain boiled over what to say. What to do.

"Look, girl, to my way of thinking this is a damn fool errand," I said as we rounded onto the too-short cross street.

"You really think that, do you?"

"I do, by God," I answered. "So, do me a favor."

"Sure, Conner. I'll do you two, if you want." A lot of mischief in those big eyes and up-twisted lips.

I shook my head, hopeless. "Try to keep it friendly. Follow my lead a bit. I'll probably lie like a tired hound dog. And don't, please, tell the guy what we're really doing."

She laughed. "That's three favors."

A quicksilver laugh, fluid, chimed through small, even teeth.

"That's one favor all tied up in a big Christmas bow."

"Then Merry Christmas, Gambler."

Maybe Windy meant yes. I hoped that was so.

Salt, rain, and wind scoured all things on Galveston Island. Add neglect to the house Windy brought me to. The place sorely needed a whitewash. Maybe a good handful of blued, asphalt shingles would not go amiss. In contrast, the front yard, despite the winter ravages, showed some care. Azaleas sentried either side of the steps in brick-lined plots. What looked like redbud trees, winter-naked but showing nubs of buds, footed by monkey grass, grew centered in the lawn either side of the flagstone walk.

Windy's gloved hand took mine as she led me up the steps. She held on to it as the other hand pulled open the ripped screen door and knocked on the small window pane. The rapping sounded muffled from her glove.

The door popped open but only enough to show a face. An old

man's face. Rheumy-eyed with dark, puffed lower lids. Veiny, blister-red nose. Angry frown. Angry jowls. His breath stank of stale coffee, beer, and cigarettes.

"What?" he rasped.

"Good afternoon, sir." Windy tried friendly.

"What?" A growl.

"We want to see your son."

The old man glared. "Who are you then?"

"My name is Susan Wright. I'm Victoria Yeats' niece."

"That's that—that woman 'round the block, right?" He made it sound like a witch's curse.

Windy nodded.

"There's no way I'd let that Jezebel have my son. I wouldn't allow it."

She passed me a meaningful glance. Arched eyebrow and all. Did the fool just say he did it?

"Victoria had a streak of wildness. Her family knew it, sir. But we are not all like that. I swear."

Don't think the old man believed her. He turned to me. "Who are you then?"

"Ted Yeats, sir," I lied. The first thing to come to mind. "Cousin to Victoria's husband."

"She's married?"

"Widowed. My cousin died of the flu back in 1918."

"Come for her funeral, did you?"

I nodded.

He harrumphed. "My kid's around back."

The door shut in our faces.

"I'm confused," Windy told me. "But did that old man just confess?"

"Came damned close."

"But, his son…" She left her thought unfinished.

Another suspect got put on my list.

"Pa just came close. A person might want to assume. It was no confession, though," I said. He stayed on the list anyway.

We got around back to see the son tossing garden tools into drawers in his garden shed. A skinny kid, in his twenties maybe. Olive skin. Black, Bakelite glasses. A permanent frown over a gray chin that would look like it needed a shave two minutes after he laid down his razor. A prominent, bobbing Adam's apple. A serious, suspicious squint came at us when he noticed us coming around the corner. Dirty coveralls over long johns. Fleece-collared work coat and calf-high rubber boots.

"Good morning," Windy sang at him. "It's Harold, yes?"

The, boy, I thought of him as boy though he might have been my age, shot her a look I could not interpret. He nodded.

She gestured to me. "This is Ted. Victoria's brother-in-law."

Harold's eyes widened. He looked even less comfortable. I stuck out a hand. After a second or two of hesitation, he put his hand on mine. On it, not in it. Cold and moist. A dead man's hand. And, if this cluck somehow turned out to be the murderer, I'd be the guy to get him to a shallow hole in a deep swamp.

"I'm sorry about Victoria. I know you liked her," Windy said. Deep sincerity in her eyes. I bought it anyway. So did he, I thought.

"She didn't like me. You know that." Were there tears welling in his eyes?

"Victoria liked you well enough, Harold. She told me so."

"Then why…" he started.

"Be easy," Windy said. "She was a new widow. Afraid of, or at least not ready, for any, uh, entanglements."

Oh, so my Cathedral statue could lie on the fly. 1918. 1925. How many years did it take for a young, pretty widow need to entangle herself?

Harold didn't appear to believe it. Actually, he appeared something else. Angry and fearful all at once. He opened his mouth as if to reply.

"Be easy. Time," Windy said. She reached out to touch the stained arm of his dirty coat. "Give it time and things will be alright. Time, Harold."

Those kinds of words got folks to bottle up. To sit on things. I wanted the dew dropper to talk.

"What happened to Victoria, Harold?" I asked. "I've heard things. She wasn't like this when she was married to my cousin."

He regarded me a moment. "I didn't know her before."

So I got nothing. Except that he made a bunch of faces I couldn't figure out. I changed the subject.

"Your garden. Beautiful come spring, I bet. Must be hard work?"

The man almost smiled.

"It is, but it's work I love," he said.

"What grows in this?" I indicated the rough table in the center of the yard. It was subdivided into six equal-sized sections.

"Strawberries first. I'm starting them midwinter. After, I'll put in marigolds. Different colors."

"Nice," I said. "I noticed you're stirring up the dirt along the fence…"

He turned to look. "Oh, yes. I'm thinking about cherry laurel. Maybe. Or, yellow jasmine."

"They'll climb up those lattices?"

"The jasmine will. Cherry laurel is more like a hedge."

"Do you grow vegetables?" Windy asked with an enthusiastic smile.

"Sure. Beans. Tomatoes. Radish sometimes. It's not a vegetable, but I might try a couple of banana trees in the back corners."

She, they, went at it for a time. A long time as it turned out. I got distracted. An old aunt of mine once told me that jasmine was poisonous.

I had to go back and talk to Doc Kennedy.

DANCING

———————————⫷⟐⫸———————————

The rich smells of coffee percolating snaked through the house. Jenny and Mai clattered around and giggled out in the kitchen. They'd promised to bring some to us when it was done. I could hardly wait.

Bobbie Lee sat waiting with me. Joe was on the floor sorting through a couple of crates of liquor. Some for the house. Some to sell around town. I'd been watching him while the wake-up fog settled out of my soul. I grinned. His tongue seemed to do most of the work as he determined which bottle went where.

"I'm with Bobbie Lee," he said to me as his eyes remained on the crates. "It's his wife that did it."

"Why do you think that?" I asked.

Bobbie Lee provided the answer. "Well, why do you think? It's usually the wife. Especially when it's poison. Just like Mai told us."

Mai once told Bobbie Lee and me of her grandmother's five husbands. Three of which died mysteriously.

"Really?" Joe looked up. "Then I'm not alone. Anyway, who do you know that might make a move against the likes of Donny Colleta?"

True enough, I thought. Colleta was top of the heap. Longtime friend of Beach Gang boss, Ollie Quinn. A real friend. They had lots of history together. Some of the Town Gang boys might have the sand. But it was all cuddles in the berry patch these days. Everybody a pal. And I hoped it stayed that way.

"I want to know about the girl," Joe said. He chinked the last of his bottles into their crates, satisfied with his sort.

"Yeah. Me too," Bobbie Lee said. "She have those lonesome legs?"

"What on God's green earth are lonesome legs?"

I turned, caught out, to see Jenny coming in with coffee. Mai trailed behind her.

"Tell us, Conner," Mai said. She put one of the steaming cups she held in front of Bobbie Lee. Kept the other for herself. She circled around to stand next to the poker table.

Jenny came over to hand me a cup. "I want to know about lonely legs, too."

I kept my lips shut.

"Lonely legs," Bobbie Lee said finally. "They're legs that are in bad need of a friend. Legs a guy wants to be friends with."

Jenny laughed.

Mai drew herself up to sit on the poker table. Making a show of it. Making a show of crossing those Asian pale legs. Way too much rounded thigh peeked out of her short, scarlet skirt.

"A woman's legs, my legs," she said. "Will only be alone when she wants them to be, boys."

I smiled at the challenge in her eyes and in her voice. And I didn't doubt the truth in her words.

"Did she? Did the girl have lonely legs?" Jenny asked, her gaze sober and even.

"Don't really know. Both times I saw her she wore pants." Looking at everybody looking at me made me think I needed to apologize. "Sorry."

Disappointed, they all turned to other business. Save for Jenny. She sat down beside me to sip at her coffee.

"You're struck by her," she said. "I see it in your eyes."

I gave my head a shake. "I gotta admit, she's a treat to look at with these tired ol' eyes."

"She's a looker, she is," Jenny agreed.

"She is."

"Sounds like you didn't have a good time."

"That damn skirt forced a meet with one of the guys that might have killed the Yeats woman."

"Not a good thing?"

"I wasn't ready."

"He the killer?"

That got a shrug from me. "Don't know. Strange guy. Gave me the heebies being in front of him, but he was a pretty mousey guy."

"Man coming up," Joe said. He must have seen something out the front window.

"Anyway, Conner, whoever said a pretty girl can't also be a damned skirt," Jenny dismissed me with a gesture.

I tried to ease my way toward the door. Mai clotted my ear with her knuckles as I passed her.

"What was that for?" I palmed the sore ear.

"That's for all the damned skirts. Even the ones in the room, you empty-skulled Paddy," she said. She still sat, crossed-legged, on my poker table, but she shared glances with Jenny.

Joe waited for a couple of raps on the wood before he opened the door. A young kid stood there in a fur-lined black flogger, shiny black brogans, and an oversized, tan newsboy cap. Young kid, maybe my age or a couple of years older. His smiling eyes glittered with self-importance.

He stepped passed Joe like he'd been invited.

"I'm here to see that famous Mick, Conner Miles," he said, hands stuffed deep into the large pockets of his flogger.

Did I trust those pockets? Could I? "Who's asking?"

"I'm Ray." He pulled out his hands. They were empty. "You him?"

"Ray who?" I asked. It seemed like the thing to do.

"Colleta."

That woke me right up. "I'm him."

"That's nice," Colleta said. His eyes roamed the room. "My uncle wants to see you. He's out in the car."

My eyes shifted over to Bobbie Lee. His widened and an eyebrow arched.

"Don't worry, Miles. I'll vag in here 'til you get back." Ray assured. Vag meant to stall around as in be a vagrant. His eyes roved over Jenny and Mai.

I made another glance at Bobbie Lee. He considered a second then gave a shrug.

"Dress warm. It's downright cold out there," Ray told me.

Big. Long. Blocky. Colleta's oversized, year-old Maxwell, with its large coach, promised roomy comfort. Though I felt far from comfortable. Two men stood on the street, close to the Maxwell's grill. One, a tricked-out chauffeur complete with chauffeur's cap and driving gloves, rocked to-and-fro, slapping his hands together, breath smoking. The other, an obvious bodyguard, huddled in his fur-collared flogger, hands deep in large pockets. When they spotted me, the both of them strolled, frowning, down the street until they were away from the car. To put me at ease, I thought, despite their harsh, suspicious stares.

"Mr. Colleta?" I asked the obvious when I opened the rear door for myself. He nodded.

Donny Colleta wore a gray, beribboned Hamburg, black buckskin gloves, and a heavy wool overcoat. Gold-rimmed cheaters made his long face look like an accountant. A darkly handsome, very Italian face. True to what I'd been told, no smile creased his face. Serious brown eyes studied me through those cheaters.

His gloved hand gestured me in and onto the over-stuffed, leather upholstered seat. He shifted to half face me.

After too long an eternity, he spoke.

"Sammy told me you were a kid."

I was less than flattered. I also knew that Sam Maceo hated to be called Sammy. He'd have to tolerate it because Colleta was a friend of Ollie Quinn, the bosses' boss of the Beach Gang.

"Sorry, Mr. Colleta. What can I do for you?"

"You can find who killed Mrs. Yeats," he said.

He pushed his cheaters up with a forefinger on the bridge. Myopic brown eyes stared at me through them. A scholar's eyes or a preacher's, with the slightest squint. But not the slightest smile.

I wondered what he saw. A dumb Paddy punk. Hunched deep in my flogger, I'd look smaller than I was. Blue around the gills from the cold. I hadn't shaved and my shoes could've used a shine. It had been a long night, filled with rank amateurs. No breakfast. Not enough coffee. I felt like a greasy-spoon lunch a half hour into a drunkard's stomach.

"I'll do that, Mr. Colleta."

"Got any ideas, yet?"

"A couple," I said. "One damn fool's been sniffing around her skirt. Another is some kind of sailor that didn't like hearing her say no."

"Sailor?"

"A foreigner. Don't know much about him yet."

"Do you know much about the other one?"

"He's a—a mouse." I grimaced at the memory of Windy dragging me over to the idiot's garden.

"A rabid mouse?" Colleta asked me mirthlessly.

I thought about that for a couple of seconds. "More like a leper mouse. If I chose this minute, I don't think I'd choose him."

"Then you should keep looking."

"Where, though, Mr. Colleta?" I swallowed and hoped I swallowed a bit of courage. "Who might want to hurt you? Or, get to you through Mrs. Yeats?"

Again, that hard stare through his cheaters.

"Most likely a lot of people. Some random marks who lost a lot of money. However, none of those would be likely to know of Victoria." Colleta turned to stare out the window. "The others, know Victoria or not, wouldn't dare."

"No one?"

He turned those eyes, steely eyes, back on me. "My men would fall upon them—and their sons—down to the ninth generation."

Sounded like one of Windy's quotes. If any of those folks could see what I sat there looking at, they would know the truth in those words. I looked for more courage but found only a cold knot in my gut.

"Mr. Colleta, with all respect, I have one more question I would like to ask you," I said.

"My wife. You think she might have killed Victoria," he said.

For the once, the man who never showed a fang, showed his fangs. A genuine smile that lit his bespectacled face.

"Mr. Miles, my wife is a traditional Sicilian wife. Taught to be so by traditional Sicilian women. Generations of them." Colleta saw my silence.

"I'm sorry, sir."

He raised a placating hand. "Were it me, I would have asked that same question."

"Thank you, Mr. Colleta."

"Two things, Miles. If you find that true and can offer proof, she will be mine to deal with. Not you. And second is that, in no way, can she know of you and your efforts in this."

Well, that was a puzzle.

"I have instructions, sir. Specific ones. But I'll try."

The man considered me for another eternity.

"Come see me when the thing's taken care of, Mr. Miles."

He looked away. I was dismissed.

Colleta's nephew must have watched from the window. He stepped from the house as I stepped from the Maxwell. When we met, he took a look at me. Not unlike his uncle, I thought.

"Sicilians, huh?" he asked.

"What?"

"I could tell my uncle made an impression on you."

"Yes, he did," I could only agree.

"My Uncle has that effect," Ray Colleta added. "Nice set up you have here."

"Thank you," I said. "Come around. Play a hand or two."

The nephew seemed to consider the offer. Reminded me a lot of his uncle.

"Nah. No thanks. I'm not a mark."

What do they call it? Umbrage? I took umbrage at that. "It's an honest game."

He shrugged and smiled. "No matter. Gambling's gambling. And gambling is for the marks."

"If you won't, you won't. Be seeing you, Donny's nephew."

"Be seeing you, Donny's Paddy."

The next day, I went to see Dr. Kennedy. Again.

"I saw jasmine growing along his fence."

"Yeah?" Doc Kennedy raised his brows.

"Jasmine's supposed to be poisonous, isn't it?"

"Well, yes. I tell you, though, it'd take a whole tub of it to kill a human being," he said. "Did you see any other plants growing there?"

"None. At least none I recognized," I said, then remembered. "I did see oleander."

"That can be a problem, if you get enough of it. What did he say he'd be growing come spring?"

"Strawberries and tomatoes. He also said he was gonna put in cherry laurel." I frowned. "Nothing sounding very bad."

"Cherry laurel, Conner. That stuff's bad news."

"So he did it, then," I said.

"He might have done it. If he knew how," Kennedy said. "If you can, find out what else our joyful gardener plays with. Nightshade. Foxglove. Cyclamen. If you can."

"I can try."

"Conner, this girl died hard. Hard. I got pictures."

Up came my detaining hand. "No pictures. Please."

I had to see some of Doc's murder scene photographs back last summer. Put a person right off their dinner. Death ain't pretty.

"She was a mess. Tore up."

"Beaten?"

"Strangely, I don't think so."

"Tumble me, Doc." I pointed to an ear, "The radio's squawking but I'm not catching the name of the soap."

"I'll count 'em up then," he held up a finger. "Her heels. All messed up. We see some like that from people who hang themselves. If they were close enough to a wall. They change their minds. Try to climb the wall."

"Jesus."

"She clawed at her neck. Chewed up her tongue. People do that when they can't breathe."

"Strangled?"

"No. None of those kinds of marks," Doc said. "There are poisons that can cause respiratory distress. Plant poisons can. Any doctors and drug stores have stuff that can—that might just do that."

"How about you? You have those kinds of poisons?"

"Drugs, Conner. Medicines. They can even be good for a person. Unless a person gets too much. And, yes, I have them where I can get to them."

"Any doctor can, yeah?"

"Yeah. They have them at most any drugstore, too."

"Well ain't that a duck's quack."

Between the gardeners, the apothecaries, and the doctors, half the damn Island might have done her in. I stood to go.

"One thing." Doc looked up at me. "Victoria Yeats' dying was a floor show, Conner. An ugly one. The woman thrashed and convulsed and shook. Moaned and gasped. Somebody watched the whole of it. Every moment."

"That's several things, Doc." I had never felt so appalled. "Are you sure about it? That someone watched?"

"I am."

"Why, for God's sake?"

"For God's sake, thank God, that's your job."

"Enough. I gotta go."

"Go to figure who watched?"

"Go to pick up a new suit. After all of this," I gestured to the stuff on his desk. "I have to go dancing."

"Hopeless. You're just hopeless, Conner," Windy told me. But she said it with a smile that was both hellish bliss and heavenly mischief.

I put my best smile on my mug. "Maybe not hopeless. Maybe hopeful."

She shook her head. "Hopeless, Gambler."

The *Raymon Candless' Roman Candle Swing Band* started yet another squealing jazz number. I surrendered. At least Windy showed no obvious limp. Yet. I took her elbow.

"Punch?" I asked.

"Punched-up punch, I'm thinking." She allowed me to walk her to the line of tables along the short wall of the Sons of Herman lodge hall.

The Lutheran Women's Auxiliary had spread out a burden of assorted cakes, muffins, cookies, and fudge. At one end were two cauldron-sized crystal bowls of blood-colored liquid. Each with a big block of ice floating around several dippers. Before the bowls sat ranks of glass tumblers, lined up with military precision.

I managed not to slop much of the punch into two glasses. I put one in her hand and took a blue cloth napkin from one of the watchful Auxiliary ladies.

"Let's duck," Windy ordered.

"Chilly out there."

"Won't be for long." She tapped my jacket pocket, getting a tenor thunk from the flask hidden there.

Windy was a beauty. Classic purity wrapped comfortably in ivory cardigan and dress. Ivory stockings and strapped shoes. Many eyes followed our stroll toward the doors. Men appraised. Women judged. I kind of wavered between flattered and afraid just being with her.

Windy's hand found my arm. She intertwined. Yes, flattered. I stayed flattered for five more steps until the girl stopped dead.

"He's there," she breathed into my ear.

I followed her eyes. Or, tried to. Just people at a dance. The band, in bottle-green tuxes and grease-slicked hair. Milling or dancing crowd. Kids mostly. Short ones, tall ones, round ones, and thin. The skirts were short and the pants with knife-sharp creases. Heels kicking, toes tapping, elbows flailing. Laughter and shouts. Kids at a dance.

Then I spotted him. A head taller than everyone else. Blond hair haloed by the stage lighting. Tailored navy uniform, but not American navy. I had to like the belled trousers that coated his butt like a Chrysler's paint job.

Bold, carved jawline easy enough to see from across the hall. Eyes hawked the room. Looking for the next conquest, I guessed. I might've been bit jaundiced, however.

"Bird of prey," Windy said, watching him as he plodded into the press of dancers.

He made a furrow clear across the floor and nabbed one of the canceled stamps, the wall flowers, on the far side.

"Nope," I said. "Vulture on a stump, more like. You, you and I, are the birds of prey, I think."

Windy smiled at that.

"Eagle or falcon? She asked.

"Shrike."

"I don't know what that is."

"A tiny bird that swoops down on its victim, then drives it onto a thorn for the kill."

"A most inglorious fowl." She grimaced.

"Glory is for preachers and army recruits, Windy. I don't think there will be much of that in what I'm doing," I said and felt the words.

She looked at me, unsaid questions in those wide eyes.

Me, I searched out Bobbie Lee. He flailed and kicked, in some form of the Lindy, with some curly-haired ginger. We caught eyes and then exchanged one of those looks we gave each other. The sorry bastard finished the dance before he made his way over.

"You see that tall blond over there at the canceled stamps?" I said. "Got him tumbled?"

Bobbie Lee drew a bead, then nodded. "Queer his racket?"

"Yep. Get in his way as best you can." I said, then added. "Don't overdo it."

He waved away my concerns and drifted into the crowd of biscuits and bun dusters. At least that's what Windy called the dancers. I was no bun duster. No, I was a corn shredder. Me and my size eleven dog kennels.

"You got him doing it, not you?" Windy asked.

"Bobbie Lee's better at things like that than I am," I said.

"Better at what, exactly?"

"At giving skirts a rush. Especially any that grabs attention from that sailor."

"Give him some competition?"

"Yeah. Rattle his cage some. Give the skirts something to think on instead of going off with him."

"In case he's the one who hurt Victoria?"

"In case." I nodded. "You ready to doctor up that punch?"

We marched our punch onto the street and soldiered around the side of the building. Out of the uncertain, wet breeze. I doctored it up from my flask. We talked to each other a little bit. Off and on. About nothing much. When Windy's teeth started clattering, I sent her in. I told her to dance with someone. Not Bobbie Lee or the sailor.

I paced the sidewalk in front of the Lodge and pretended to drink the half inch of red liquid still in the cup. Pretended I believed what I hoped might happen would happen. Forty-five or so minutes later it did.

The sailor came out lighting a skinny cigarillo. Awkwardly, because he held his own cup of punch.

I turned and smiled at him.

"Sailor?" I asked the obvious.

He pulled his smoke from the fingers holding the glass, took a drag, and made an 'of course' gesture.

"Not the American navy?"

"*Nej*—no," he said. The foreign part sounded something like nay. "I Sveed-ish."

The last part was so sing-song I thought he was putting me on.

"You like it here in America?"

"*Ja. Ja.* Is good, Galveston."

"Pretty girls?" I asked. Tried hard to make the question sound like simple talk.

"*Ja.* Pretty girls here." Again with the sing-song.

I smiled agreement and sipped a touch of my punch. He took a sip of his.

"Got something good in that punch?" I gestured at his cup.

It took a second for the man to get my meaning. "*Nej.* Only—only this is."

"Want something?"

Another moment. He appeared interested but wary.

"Bootlegger?" he singsonged. "I want nothing to buy."

"No. No. I'm not selling. Let's consider it a Christmas present." I pulled out my flask.

He held out his cup and was happy to take as much as I would pour.

He took it like a man. No bad face. No cough. I was impressed.

"Nice." He raised his glass.

"So, you swab decks? Shovel coal? What?" I asked. Tried to prod him a little.

"*Ja, ja.* You Americans. Know nothing about nothing." He shook his head. "I am—how do you say—I am medical officer."

I put surprise on my face and hoped he bought it. "You Swedes carry medical officers on your ships?"

"*Ja.* Some. The ship's out for long voyage."

"How long?"

"Months. Depends on cargo. On ports."

"Your men get sick a lot?" I asked, fishing for what drugs he might use.

"*Nej. Nej.* Not much. Broke fingers. Bruise. What you call it—busted gut." He touched at his groin.

"Hernia?"

"*Ja.* That."

"You staying here long? Through Christmas?"

"Maybe. Maybe New Years. Maybe next week. Don't know. Depends on Captain. On cargo."

I felt some pressure then. Next week as worst thing. I needed more time. Ouch.

"Wouldn't think there'd be much in Texas in the winter. What y'all loadin'?"

The Swedish sailor struggled as he listened. I figured he wasn't used to y'all yet.

"Oh, *ja.* We wait for dried corn. Hides. I think some cotton too."

"Lots of dances between now and New Year. Lots of skirts," I said and noticed some puzzlement. "Skirts. Girls. Lots of girls. Good waiting."

"Oh, *ja.* Good."

Good? If he would stay docked that long. I had to get on that ship.

SOUTH WIND

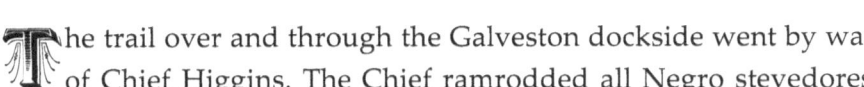

The trail over and through the Galveston dockside went by way of Chief Higgins. The Chief ramrodded all Negro stevedores, porters, and landsmen who worked the piers.

Kind of had a love/hate relationship with the man off and on since last summer. A useful man to know, he and his underling that called himself Laq. I knew just how to get to know him better. With Bobbie Lee in tow, I stuffed several wads of double sawbucks in several pockets and took the Studebaker to Higgins' office.

Nothing special about it. A corner space in an old brownstone building, faded and salt-stained. No sign over a door that needed painting. Big, dingy windows.

A tinny bell hung on the wall above the door jangled as I entered. A lot of grimy nothing smelling of old dust, old cement, and old paint. A couple of scruffy, tired men sat on two of the mismatched chairs lined up in the center of the cracked, tiled floor. Their weary eyes came up to stare the stare Negros gave to white men.

Big, gruff Chief Higgins stood over the desk where his skinny assistant, Laq, shuffled at some papers. They looked up at me with the same stare. The Chief, looking like he'd been born to calloused hands and sore feet, took a couple of seconds to recognize me.

"I declare, look what Paddy rag the mange cat done drug in," he said. A slow smile drew up the corners of his ample lips.

"Morning, Chief," I said. I stepped in and closed the door with a respectful thump. That bell jangled again. "Can you spare me a minute or two, please?"

He looked down at Laq.

"Listen to this. Please, he says. Did he say please the last time you saw him?" He turned those hard, liquid brown eyes back on me.

"Nah, he didn't, Mister Higgins, suh," Laz slurred.

I wasn't really sure when I last saw Laq. The time I remember, though, had me rousting the poor sap and giving Chief Higgins' office files a good rifling. I'd not been nice about it.

"This time I'm asking with a please," I said. But I didn't say it with a smile.

Higgins pretended to consider it a minute. He shrugged a nod. "Come on back."

A short hallway, crowded with filing cabinets, ushered us into more of them that seemed like sentries, half-blocking any view on his cluttered, beat up oaken desk. He gestured right, to a chair I had to slither around the cabinets to get to. He went left to a Victrola on what once had been a wash basin., cranked the thing up, and sat the needle on a 78, to play soulful, bass sax.

He sat. "Can you hear me over that noise?"

I nodded.

"Good. You can, they can't. What's this all about? Somebody else out to kill you?"

That had been the subject of our last meeting.

"Need your help for a thing," I said.

"My help ain't free, Paddy."

"I know," I patted my jacket over its breast pocket.

He put a sharp eye on my hand.

"What 'cha want?"

"You got a Swedish ship loading cargo out there?" I chinned toward the piers.

"Might."

"Know when it's due to ship out?"

"Might."

I puffed out my exasperation. "Damn, Chief."

"Four or five days. Ten days. Depends. What's this all about?"

"I want to slow that up."

"How long?"

"Long. Christmas, maybe. New Year's."

"Jesus Christ's black bottom, Paddy!"

"If it can get done, you're the man that can get it done."

"That's a big ask."

I felt the press of the five twenties in my breast pocket. "I got a century ready to go."

That put a speculative glint in his eye. But it also marked me.

"That might make the rent. Maybe. Something like this though—I can't do it alone."

"How much for the hired help?"

That took another hundred, fished from another pocket.

"The ship is called the *Sydvind*." He pronounced it Sooth-vend. "I think it means the South Wind. Follow me out. I'll show it to you."

The South Wind looked a well-found ship. As far as I could tell, anyway. The freshest paint job in harbor. The gangway leading into the thing got most of my attention. I thanked the Chief with another sawbuck and walked back to the Studebaker full of thought, plans, and possibilities. Most discouraged me. I wanted on that ship.

Two nights later, two bums sat in a Studebaker parked a half a block down from the dance. My plan, such as it was, began.

The clothes I wore back when I collected coins from Maceo slot machines squeezed at my nooks and crannies. I'd thickened up some since then. But they had the tone of a working man, if I wore the too-small newsboy cap borrowed from Yuli. Bobbie Lee, beside me in the car, had scruffed up as well.

We watched the kids, hand-in-hand, and their chaperons hauling baskets of snacks march into the hall. Muted jazz pounded through the walls, reaching all the way to the car.

"There he is." Bobbie Lee pointed.

Our Swedish mark sauntered up from the dark shadows of Mechanic Street. From the general direction of the docks. Even from where we parked, I saw his eyes fixed on the swaying hips of some girls headed toward the thrumming jazz pulses.

"Soon as he's inside we'll head out," I said.

"You really think this'll work?"

"If you got something better, serve it on up."

"Nope. Not me," Bobbie Lee said. "Anyway, I like you being the boss. Makes everything your fault.

A guy could almost hear my eye roll. I pushed the starter and snapped my foot off the clutch. The Studebaker gave a sharp jerk and the engine coughed dead.

"I changed my mind on the boss thing," Bobbie Lee said.

"Let me try this again."

Being a touch more gentle got us to the piers fairly quick. Had to sweep the docked ships with the spot light to find the *Sydvind*. Lights showed aboard, but I saw no crewmen. I killed the engine.

Before we fished our two crates from the rear seat, I beeped the horn a couple of times. By the time we reached the foot of the gangway, a hard-eyed blond sailor looked down on us.

"*Vah? Vah vill du?*" he called.

I chinned at the crate hugged into my chest. "Medical supplies. Delivery."

If what we carried could be called that. Bobbie Lee told me that his Confederate Corporal grandfather set great store in brandy when laudanum ran out. So I made brandy on the cheap. Twice distilled, homemade gin, some molasses for sweet and color, water, and a touch of Jenny's perfume to make it taste flowery like brandy. Bottles came easy enough. We got labels from the guy that made the gin. It was his recipe. At least, I hoped, no one would go blind from it.

"*Vah?*" The man called again. Another crewman joined him.

"What's he saying?" Bobbie Lee hissed at me.

"What."

"What's he saying?" he asked again.

"What. I think he's asking what we want." I turned back to the Swede. "Delivery. I gotta take this to—to wherever your doctor keeps stuff."

"*Vah will du?*" The two sailors started down the noisy metal gangway.

"Medical supplies. Medicine." I repeated. Louder. Foreigners understood stuff said loud enough.

"What want? What want?" the new arrival asked.

"We have this," I chinned at the crate again. "Take to doctor. Doctor."

I put the crate down and mimed things I hoped doctors did. "Doctor. Doctor. Understand?"

"Ah. *Ja, ja*. Lay-care-ray," he said. "Lay-care-ray. Dak tare."

"Yes," I nodded, then turned to Bobbie Lee. "Get out one of the good stuff."

Bribe or reward, which ever might be needed. Two bottles of the real stuff rested in his crate, just in case. He prized one out. Not dropping the crate, thank God.

"For you," he said.

The one that spoke a little English took it up and beamed a smile.

"*Tack*. Thank. I thank." He gestured behind himself. "*Komma*. You come. I show."

The sailor led us up the gangway. There wasn't much above the main deck that I could see. A two-story structure, the glassed-in bridge above, and something lined with round port holes below. This fronted one huge smoke stack. Two high mast-looking things, fore and aft, holding up long cranes. Lots of lines and rigging surrounding them. The whole thing stank of tar and burnt fuel oil.

Then we went down steps to a lower deck. Then down again into the bowels of the ship. A new smell, fresh paint, added to all the others. None smeared me as I bumped along whatever they called the endless walls aboard the ship. I could feel the throb of engines and the breath of stale air that came through the deck and from the handful of vents. The ship was empty and felt eerie.

Our Swede finally stopped at a closed wooden door. He tapped several times. No answer. Good.

He gestured and said something that sounded like 'her.'

"*Her. Her,*" he said. He opened the door.

"Here?" I asked.

"*Ja. Ja.*"

We went in. Sat the crates on the deck. Small room. Small desk, with a small lamp, and a small chair. Another chair that looked like it belonged in a barber shop. Or a dentist's office. Two glass-fronted cabinets, and several banks of shelves, all crowded with medicines. Just what I wanted to see. Needed to see.

"I got this," I said. I began to unload the bottles. We would keep the crates. "Get him to crack open that bottle you gave him."

I wanted the sailor's attention somewhere other than in this room.

Bobbie Lee stepped into the hall and started his pitch. I put my bottles on the deck and then my eyes on the medicines.

QUICKSILVER

L isten to that thing purr." I sipped on my Irish as Dutch drove off in his Nash Roadster.

"Sweet. That straight six can fly," Bobbie Lee agreed.

"Sweet deal, too, I heard."

"Five hundred and a case of Canadian."

"Over paid." I took another sip.

"This is what you saw?" Jenny asked me as she hunched over the scribbled paper.

"Saw other things but not everything had labels in English."

"Hmm, I wonder what the man thought of all his poxy crewmen." She seemed to speculate, not really asking.

"Poxy?"

"Cinnabar," Jenny said. "Used to cure syphilis. Or quicksilver is. The mercury cure. And you get that from this stuff.

"How?" Bobbie Lee asked.

Jenny shrugged no. "The chloroform is needed for surgeries. Then there's the chloral hydrate…"

"So what's with that?"

"You don't know?"

Bobbie Lee's turn to shrug.

"I bet you that you and Connor used it, or would if you could."

"Dime on my dollar, she's gonna tell us what for if we ask her," I said.

She looked all studious and serious, bent over the sheet of paper. Fetching in her brassy, long-sleeved jacket, trimmed in black at throat and cuffs. Her black ribbon headband, with a gold broach affixed over her delicate ear. She peeked at me without raising her head.

"You would call it a Mickey," she said.

Bobbie Lee regarded her a moment. "She's right. I might just use it, if I had reason enough and a way to slip it in."

He let out a huge yawn. And looked twelve doing it.

"Had enough?" I asked him.

"Yep. Enough." He turned to Jenny. "Wanna ride?"

"You didn't see my car outside, I guess. Thanks, but I'll get myself home." She made her small, magic smile at him, gratitude-scented almost.

As he grabbed his coat and newsboy cap to walk out the front door, Jenny studied my roughed up scrap of paper. The lighted Christmas tree glowed and smelled of pine. My large space heater hissed the smell of burnt gas and scorched fire bricks. Jenny's *Soir-de-Paris* ghosted over me. I could see the vein at her throat pulse slowly as I felt my own throb.

She spent some more time reading the list, then folded it once and set it on the table.

"You think he did it?" she asked.

"Don't really know. Too soon. Though, looking at that list, he had the tools."

She shook her head. "Whoever did this has to be one twisted up son of a devil mother."

"That's my thought, too. I guess. But, I still have to consider that it might not have been a son of anybody's mother."

"What woman could…?"

I held up a hand.

"Once, Mai told me that poison is a woman's weapon,"

"Colleta's wife?"

"Colleta's wife."

Jenny looked thoughtful for a moment. Whatever she thought about, however, she passed over. Instead, she took up a deck of cards and started that one-handed deck cutting she was so good at.

"How are things going with the black ball pennant?" she asked, mischief turning up the corners of her mouth.

"The what?"

"A red, triangular flag, with a big black ball in its center. It means a gale's going to blow. I meant, how are things going with Windy Wright?"

"Okay," I chuckled. And maybe grimaced as I thought. "Well, she blows a storm sure enough. Why? Do I look weather-beaten or something?"

Jenny laughed.

"Kind of, yes."

I shook my head. "What can I say, the skirt is real nice to look at."

"Yep. She's that." What I thought was going to be a nod turned into an eye roll. "Of course, I always thought she had bit of devil in those over-big eyes of hers."

I guess there was Satan in the way Windy lit up on seeing the dew dropper in his garden.

"Did she have lonely legs to make friends with?" she asked.

"Don't know. The girl wore pants."

"Buy me a drink?"

"You got it, young lady."

The kitchen seemed like a long way away, but that's where I kept my personal stash of Irish whiskey. Some went into a couple of tumblers. A splash of water went into Jenny's. She'd told me that a bit of water made better sipping. I hadn't bought into that myself.

When back through the door, I found Jenny sitting on the couch, half draped over the padded arm, her shoes off and feet on the coffee table. Close to the fire.

"Thanks much." She smiled and took the glass.

I sat and draped myself across the other arm of the couch. Stretched my legs toward the fire. Sipped at the whiskey. Sighed a contented sigh.

"This is nice," I said. "Nice way to end a day that I'm glad is over."

Jenny looked into the blue flames. Thoughtful.

"The day is over, huh Paddy? You've decided that, have you?"

I coughed, puzzled. "Just something to say."

Sitting up, I put the half a drink on the coffee table. Jenny's hand took a hold on my forearm. She moved me back, not to drape crosswise on the couch. She turned. Her legs came up to lay across my lap.

"I have lonely legs tonight. They need a friend, I think."

An awful lot of those legs showed on my side of the hem of her dress.

As God is my witness, there are few things in life better than the feel of a lady's thigh sheathed in silk. My hand felt right at home placed there.

But, young as I was, I already knew that women wanted more than just that. So I let my other hand slide lightly along her shin to work at her heels, soles, and toes.

Jenny let out a long, pleasured sigh.

"You are a magician yourself, Conner," she breathed. "I'm not sure I truly appreciated that before."

She raised her knees to rest her feet on my legs. The hem of her skirt dropped down some to show the knotted hose tops and just a bit of naked skin. I let my hand play down to touch the contrast of silk and flesh.

"There is magic and there is magic, Jenny."

She smiled with just a touch of mischief. I let my fingers tickle at her inner thigh. By the look of her closed eyes, it was nice for us both.

"I'd take another drink," she said. Her feet left my legs. Her thigh left my hand.

When I returned with the refilled drinks, Jenny stood facing me. She lifted a hand to her earring. I lowered my gaze. Chill air had gotten to her nipples. They seemed to beckon to me through the fabric of her clothes. She noticed my gaze and looked down at herself.

"Oh," she said. With a smile, thank God.

I gave the smallest chuckle.

"Magic, Jenny," I said.

She shot me a look I couldn't figure out. Then she turned and looked at me over her shoulder.

"Aren't you coming?" she asked.

I wasn't asked twice. When I entered the darkness of my bedroom, Jenny had both hands at an ear removing her jewelry. Her glittery brain binder came off next.

She laid them on my dresser. "I think you should undress me now."

I didn't need a second ask then either. Jenny's overshirt had no buttons. I pulled it from her shoulders and lowered it until her arms were uncovered. I listened to the quiet caress of the fabric as it slid along her skin. In all reverence, I laid it atop her jewelry.

She turned to show me the row of buttons down the back of her dress. A straight-line dress with a knotted sash wrapping low on her hips. It was good that the buttons were black, so I could make them out in the dark.

With the last one undone, she turned to me, shrugged the thing from her shoulders, and let it fall to the floor. Her white slip, not quite as short as her dress, fairly glowed. And those winter-assaulted nipples strained against the silk.

She reached to work the buttons of my shirt and rocked me gently to pull the shirttails from my pants. Her turn to lift the shirt from my shoulders. It fell to the floor. More pulling and rocking on belt and pants buttons. It fell down around my ankles.

She waited.

When I figured out what she waited for, I hooked two fingers beneath the straps of her slip. Then it was just Jenny in her hose and her breasts that seemed to reach out for me.

She sat on the bed and raised a leg up for me. I untucked the knots of her stocking and removed it ever so slowly. Same with the other one.

"No man comes into a bed with me in his socks, Conner," she teased.

When they joined the pile on the floor, she pulled me down next to her.

In the quiet of winter, our hands, our lips and our tongues sought out all of our lonely places, and made friends in the dark.

CHAIRS

Jenny headed out early.

"A lady can't be found in the morning wearing the same clothes from the night before," she said, smiled, and made a raspy tickle under my chin. "Shave, Paddy. See you tonight."

I watched her leave. I'd shave, but not before coffee. A lot of it.

Bobbie Lee showed up at the kitchen door just as I turned off the fire below the speckled blue, enameled percolator.

"Got enough for me?"

"Already got your mug out."

I poured for us both. Bobbie Lee came over for his.

"Jesus, man, you smell good," he said with a leer.

I smelled of cigarette smoke and sex.

"Yeah, well," I groaned. "It's early."

"Too early."

"What's got you out at this hour?" I asked.

"I'm just a restless soul."

He was at that, thinking of it. He followed me out and sat on the couch. I struck a match to the space heater and cranked the fire high. The big lounge chair by the couch sat there inviting me, so I sprawled into it.

"Can I have one of your butts?" he pointed to the half-full deck on the coffee table.

"Only if you pass one to me."

He took out two, stuck them in his mouth, and lit them. One he passed to me. His, he inhaled deeply and let out a cloud with a contented sigh.

"There are few things better than your first smoke after a meal," he said.

"You eat already?"

"Eggs, bacon, and toast over at the greasy spoon by my house. What's its name? I forget."

I sure didn't know but I envied him his bacon. I scratched my stubble.

Bobbie Lee grinned. "So, you and Jenny, huh? I'm impressed."

Tried to hide the smile, but grinned anyway.

"Who Says?"

Bobbie Lee laughed. "Won't rat yourself out, huh?"

"My mamma raised a gentleman," I lied.

He rolled his eyes.

"Don't serve out your crap at me, boy." I said.

"Well, I guess we won't be seeing a lot of you two anymore. What we gonna do?"

"Don't fret yourself. Jenny and I talked about it. Agreed that the game's the most important."

"That means Jenny's not serving up more of Jenny anytime soon, you know."

I made an obscene gesture. He made another eye roll.

"Saw Joe at breakfast. Said he'd be over directly."

"Good."

He arrived while I bathed, scraped my razor over my face, and dressed. The crisp-ironed khaki shirt and pants he wore bore a fairly close resemblance to a utility man's uniform. Even had a name sewn atop the left pocket. A pile of coats, two or three, rested on the couch next to him. A newsboy cap and a pork pie hat sat on the coffee table in front of him.

I hated pork pie hats. Ridiculous things with a flat top and a round, upturned brim. They always looked too small for the head that wore them.

"Stupid looking things," I said, eyeing the hat.

"Silly as hell, for sure. But people see the hat and don't always look at the face," he said. Joe's wiry red hair skewed this way and that, and his freckles made his face glow as pink as my fresh-shaved cheeks felt.

"Good enough, I reckon. You're clear on what you gotta do?"

"Shadow the dew dropper. Don't get caught doing it."

"You feel good about being able to do that?"

"Don't worry, Conner. This is something I do well," Joe said. "Anyway, I'm a Jew. There's few things Jews do better than be invisible. It'll be alright."

"Bobbie Lee?" I asked, finally noticing his not being in the room.

"Out back," Joe said.

"Throwing knives?"

"What else. The man likes his blades."

I shook my head. Loved them, more like. My blades, too. Every knife in this place could split a hair lengthwise if it fell on it one end first.

From the French doors, I could see him out there in his shirt-sleeves throwing his collection of butcher knives at a ragged plank he'd nailed to the live oak. Over handed. Under handed. Side armed. He flicked one back-handed from close to his waist as I opened the door. Never a miss.

"Hey man, damn. You almost ruined my throw," he barked.

"Never happen. All lumber thinks you are the Grim Reaper." I shook my head. "I'm making tracks."

"Where you going?"

"Out," I said. He'd remember, given a minute.

"I like out. Out is a good place to go," He nodded and headed over to gather his collection.

I left him to it.

My first stop was Doc Kennedy's, despite not wanting to go there. But I needed some stuff. At least the day was warmer. Damp and breezy, but almost comfortable. As Galveston was apt to do. Hoped it would last.

Coming up L Street toward Victoria's house meant that I came up to that black Ford with my old friend, the cannon carrier. I braked the Studebaker up next to him and slipped the transmission into neutral.

The man's gaze stayed hard and suspicious even after the flicker of recognition. I opened the window.

"Having fun yet?"

He grimaced as he pondered just what I meant.

A finger came up to push his fedora higher on his brow.

"Oh, it's all go here. Confetti and balloons," he said. "You know, trying to get old acquaintances forgot. Not having much luck though."

"Well, I'm one big forget-me-not." I grinned at him.

"So it seems."

"Anything?" I asked.

He shook his head no. "Some lowlid crasher pulled up to the corner, got out, stumped off 'round the corner."

"Pork pie hat?" I asked. That might be Joe.

The tough guy nodded.

"Didn't show any interest in the house." Meaning Victoria's.

"Yeah. He won't. Or shouldn't," I said. "Got him on something down the block. Try not to queer his racket if you can."

Actually, I wanted to say leave him the hell alone, but using that kind of tone seemed like not the thing to do.

"Make sure I don't be tripping over him then," he growled.

I flipped him a haphazard salute, clutched the Studebaker into gear, and hummed on down to Victoria's.

Abandoned buildings creep me out anytime. A dizzy smell of emptiness. A silence I could hear. A deeper stillness because of what happened.

My footsteps echoed too loud. So I plopped into Victoria's over-stuffed lounge chair. Rich green cushions and wraparound walnut back and arms wanted to swallow me whole. I wondered if Victoria's ghost populated the thing. An unforgettable chill flooded my gut.

"Now, now, darlin'," I said, hoping her spirit wouldn't mind the familiarity. "You want me to find the guy that did this, don't you?"

For some strange reason, the silence in the room struck me like the house had something to say, but couldn't find its voice. Hair actually rose from the nape of my neck.

I got up from that damned chair and moved to the couch. With the ribbon-tied, manila folder Doc Kennedy gave me.

I left it tied because of what was in it.

The room was as I remembered it. Lots of Art Deco furniture. Lots of glittery stuff. Lots of garish colors. Victoria must have liked lots and lots.

The gauzy, pastels portrait of near-naked Windy no longer sat its place on the mantel. I wondered about it. Wondered if it found its place somewhere in the Opera House.

First in that cursed folder was the picture of the room as the police found it. Without the body. That was the second picture in the folder. I left it there.

Something was weird about the room. Someone, the killer, had moved the chair. Forward and at an angle. In front of the open space below the fireplace. As if to watch, just as Doc Kennedy thought. The coffee table was screwy, though. A corner pulled forward at a slant. To get to move the chair maybe. I would have pushed it back again. Did the killer want to rest a coffee cup on it as he watched Victoria die?

The stark, black-and-white photo didn't show one.

My big, right shoe scuffed up to the edge of the coffee table. I pushed it forward until it seemed to be at the same angle as in the photo.

The thing blocked the chair. It took some furniture moving to get the chair and the table to align something like the photo. To me, that meant the chair came out first.

The table went back, and I sat in the chair a second time. Not ghostly this time. The chair behaved, thank God.

Couldn't pull out the heavy table one-handed. So with some

huffing and puffing, scene-of-the-crime was reproduced.

I sat. I looked at the empty floor.

Why did the killer do this? What did he see?

With a leaden reluctance, I fished the other photo from Kennedy's folder.

Again, the stark contrasts of a police portrait. No corpse has any dignity. Even ones with their clothes still on.

At arm's length, Victoria looked like a huge splatter on a wooden floor. Not pretty even then.

Closer—even less so. The killer laid the poor woman bare. Her robe, white in the photo, splayed open like ragged wings, its top bunched against bare shoulders. Her right foot was pulled up to rest next to her left knee. Her arms spread, akimbo, from her body. Her right hand, palm up, rested next to her ear. Her left hand, clinched in a fist, lay down but away from her hip. The only remaining secrets left to Victoria were the parts of her arms still in the crumbled sleeves of her robe.

I remembered other pictures I'd seen of Victoria. Pictures Windy showed me. A woman more handsome than pretty. An eager smile. Direct, lively eyes. Death is ugly.

Scared of what I'd see, I tried to see Victoria on that stretch of floor. To see her alive there. Writhing. Hurting. Maybe begging.

Instead, I saw Jenny there. Instead I saw Windy there.

Couldn't shake those visions. Even after I jerked back and forced my stare anywhere but the floor.

Made it worse when I squeezed closed my eyes. Something worse than the ghost in the chair grabbed at me.

Another look. Made with a force of will. Just floor. Just emptiness. No Victoria. No Windy. No Jenny.

"What did you see, monster?" I mumbled.

Rattling sounds came from the door. A key inserted. I had not locked it behind me. The door knob, crystal on the inside, turned and the door slid open a couple of inches.

"Gambler?" a fearful whisper. Windy's whisper. "You here?"

"Better than even odds I am."

Green eyes came around and looked first at me, then the room.

"You come over here to rearrange furniture?" she asked, arching eyebrows.

I leaned forward and placed chin on palm.

"Sorry," I said, though I'm sure I didn't sound all that apologetic.

"You don't sound good." She stepped inside but kept a hand on the door knob. She did wonders for the tailored black skirt and military cut jacket and blouse.

"Not having my best day."

She closed and locked the door.

"Well, what are you doing here?"

"Trying to figure this guy out," I said.

"By scrambling the room?"

"This is pretty much like it was when the coppers showed up. Victoria would have been there." I pointed. "I'm sitting where the guy sat. Don't know what he was doing with the table."

"Okay." She sounded puzzled.

"I'm trying to see what he saw."

"He saw a girl with most of her clothes gone."

"Why do you think that?"

"Come on, Gambler, men like looking at girls. Especially girls wearing nothing but their skin," Windy said, almost matter-of-fact simple.

I looked up at her, seeing again, in my mind, the images of Victoria, Jenny, and Windy herself, there on the floor. In nothing but their skin. Hurting. Begging. Didn't mention that, though.

"Not what I meant. He watched for a long time, and it couldn't have been pretty. Why? What was he after?"

"You're watching it right now. Down in some garbage corner of your brain. I can see it. Ask yourself, just why are you watching?" she told me, then held up a restraining hand. "Don't answer. Don't want to hear it from my favorite trouble boy. Anyway, you're overthinking it."

"Maybe," I said. But I didn't think so. What happened on that stark floor was more than some fool checking out a naked lady.

"Leave off, Conner. Take a rest. You want me to crank up the Victor Victrola?"

"Good idea, Windy. Want me to pour us a couple?"

"I should like that of all things. As long as it won't cause me to go blind."

"Only the best goes in my flask."

"Give me a splash with it, will you?" She put a record on the turntable, gave the crank some turns, and a heavily over-toned tenor's warble filled the room.

When I returned from the kitchen with the drinks, Windy was sitting on the couch arm. A woman's challenge and a woman's invitation in her eyes. In her smile.

I gave the drink to her. I had to turn the chair back around to face her.

"To Victor Victrola," she said and raised her glass.

"To Victor." I raised mine as I looked at her.

Windy had draped herself across the couch. A lot of knee showed from beneath the hem of her skirt. A lot of shin. Nice knees. Nice shins. Legs softened by translucent, silk hose.

Couldn't help wondering if those legs were lonely. Wondering if they needed a friend.

She stopped looking at me look at her. Like she was letting me do so undisturbed. The mischievous challenge left her eyes too. Our erstwhile tenor launched into a silly piece about some stupid, want-to-be lover trying to work his way into some skirt's heart. We sipped our whiskey. Afternoon slipped into early evening.

Windy looked at me again. "I still say you look wore out. You could take me to a movie. If you want. Do you good."

"That sounds nice," I started, then drained the last drops from my drink. "But remember, I work nights."

"Always trying to be the Gambler, aren't you?"

"Most of the time," I agreed.

"Well, you've been asked." She put her feet on the floor then crossed her legs. The challenge came back into her eyes. "I may not ask again."

"Maybe next time, I'll ask you." I stood.

"Maybe I'll say yes," she said.

"You want me to walk you out?"

"No, Conner. Think I'll listen to some records before it gets too late."

I turned to go but turned back.

"So you think it's as simple as some nasty weasel watching a skirt dressed in nothing but her skin?"

"Almost that simple, yes."

Windy made a to-do of crossing her other leg and looked at me as I watched her do it.

"Yes. Almost that simple, Gambler."

QUESTIONS

Bobbie Lee sat back in his chair, arms crossed, lips in a wry smirk, and just shook his head slowly.

"You know, the girl wasn't asking you to any movie, don't you?" Jenny said. I couldn't figure the expression on her mug.

Only Jenny, Bobbie Lee, and the dawn glow surrounded me at the poker table.

Bobbie Lee's hair rioted on his skull where Mai tousled it on her way out. She'd left with one of the rounders that played the night away. The rounder with all the luck. Bobbie Lee, comfortable and complacent in shirt sleeves and suspenders, never minded Mai's chosen profession. And when she came back, and she always did, he was always there.

The stone, centered on the black ribbon brain binder and centered above her eyebrows, glittered as Jenny watched me. She sat composed and comfortable in sea-green cashmere as she too watched me. Still unreadable. Her fingers, unwatched, played smooth magic tricks with a deck of cards.

"Not for going to the movies," she repeated.

"Jenny's right, you know." Bobbie Lee nodded.

I rasberried my exasperation, wet and juicy, into the air. "Not my point."

Right then, I hated both of them.

They shared a glance and a grin.

"That you're thinking at all about it, is overthinking it," Bobbie Lee said. "It don't matter a damn. He, or she, did it. It got done. Don't need no thinking."

"Still stuck on Colleta's wife, huh?" I asked him.

He shrugged. "Mai thinks that. She's done thinking, too."

"Why are you putting yourself through this, Conner?" Jenny asked. She saw the look I flashed her, so she held up a hand. "Just a question."

"Because what happened in that house—on that floor—why it happened, might tell me who the hell did it."

Bobbie Lee uncrossed his arms and leaned forward, elbows on his knees.

"Well," he said. "Did it tell you who didn't do it?"

Jenny made a face. "Took me a minute to figure it out, but what he said has some sense to it."

"Did it?" I asked, because I couldn't find any.

"It did, my friend," Bobbie Lee said. "My pa, bless his drunken heart, told me that if I wasn't gettin' right answers, I'd been askin' the wrong questions."

I guessed that should have made sense. Figured it was me, not him. Too tired.

"Yeah," Jenny added. "Try asking yourself different ones."

"Maybe I should."

What different questions?

"Let's call this day over," Jenny told Bobbie Lee.

He took the hint. We watched him until he was out the door.

"We can call it done, too. Let's go slither under a pile of blankets." Jenny took my hand.

I tried hard to remember how naked I got. Tried hard to remember how naked Jenny got. And I almost sensed her body warming as she pressed against me. The last thing I was aware of that morning was her protective arm snaking its way over me.

If new and different questions came up in my dreams, I didn't remember them.

When Jenny woke me by rapping knuckles on the bedroom door, she was dressed and trying to slip on her shoes.

"Joe just pulled in." She fumbled on the last shoe. "I'll let him in on my way out. Made you bacon and toast. Coffee. Don't let it get cold."

She blew me a kiss.

I threw on last night's clothes. They smelled of cigar smoke and Jenny's perfume. Joe sat on the couch with both hands wrapped around a mug of coffee.

I got my coffee, then levered the space heater hotter before sitting opposite my wire-haired crew member.

"Not as cold out there than it has been," he said.

The sun had put a nice, straw-gold glow on the winter-burnt grass out back. Made me blink as I looked out through the French doors.

"What time is it?"

Joe looked over my shoulder at the clock on the mantel, that I was too groggy to twist and look at.

"About two," he said. "I got stuff about that sap."

"Clue me."

"Our bohunk, at least I think his ancestors started out from east of Germany, going by the name, is a lonesome guy. Mostly he stays home—alone..."

"Well, his patter don't sparkle, for damn sure."

"What?"

"He's not the smoothest conversationalist." I shrugged.

"There is a joint he goes to."

"Joint?"

"Sort of. General store that's got some slots and a couple of billiard tables in the back."

"He plays pool, huh?

Joe shrugged. "It's different from what I know. No pockets. Only a couple or four balls. That's why I said billiards, not pool. The man that owns it sells pails of beer out his back door. Sour stuff, but it's got a head on it."

"That's how you got an eyeball on Harold, I guess."

"Good guess." Joe grinned. "There's something else."

I waited.

"The sap's father got hauled out to the hospital this morning."

"Yeah?" I remembered that the miserable old man came that close to saying he did it.

"Yeah." The scatter of freckles on Joe's face broke out in another grin. "And, they don't expect him to come out of it alive."

What Joe giveth, Joe taketh away.

"How do you know this?"

"Saw the meat wagon pull up. Saw the white coats lug that man out. Even saw ol' Harold left standing in his yard looking all lost and stuff," Joe said.

"Okay. But how did you know about his dad's chances?"

"My Uncle Zev. He's a doctor up there. I asked."

Not the best news, really. It was a reach for sure, but that old man might have killed Victoria. Or, knew who did. Like his son, maybe.

"If I can get in to him, can he talk to me?"

"Not the way my uncle figures it. Harold's daddy's close to gone."

"Damn."

"Such a mouth. Do you kiss your sister with that mouth?" Joe teased.

I chuckled. "Not since you did."

Drew, Victoria Yeats' friend, introduced me to Windy's parents. Me and Ray Colleta. She introduced us as their escorts. Emphasis on the escorts. Not dates.

The two of us stood to shake the offered hands.

"Are you enjoying yourselves?" Mrs. Wright, elegant as a dance teacher would be in her bespangled and beaded Blue ball gown, asked. Her eyes were on me when she spoke.

"Yes, ma'am. Very much." I pasted on my best smile, even it was a bald-faced lie.

This was a dinner-and-dance fundraiser for a battery of Arts groups. And it was held at the opulent Hotel Galvez. Rich Christmas glitz. Rich table settings. Rich sparkling people. Even an orchestra playing under the dining room chatter.

To match the dazzle of Windy and Drew, Colleta and I wore tuxes. His tailored. Mine a somewhat roomy rental. And I felt as out of place as a bug in the cake icing.

Windy's father gave me a look like I wasn't fooling him a minute.

"You children will stay for the dancing, I presume?" he asked with a voice like a pool ball rolling around in an empty whiskey barrel. An acting teacher's voice.

This was supposed to be another night of me being hopeless at another dance, with Windy grinning at me and Bobbie Lee interfering with Poul the sailor. A night where my biggest concern would be keeping Poul from taking some girl off somewhere. Just in case. But tonight, it was just me and Windy at this gala.

I didn't know it'd be different until Ray Colleta, Donny's nephew, showed up at my door. No preamble. Just told me to grab some cash, and he was to drive me to a tux rental place. There was a wingding, and Windy thought it time that I debuted in society. Whatever the hell that meant.

It meant, I found out, that Windy and I would go with Drew and Ray to attend a gala.

"Of course, we're having a great time, sir," Ray told Windy's father. "Looking forward to being with you."

"No, no." Wright shook his head. "That's for you young people. There's cocktails and conversation for the old folks up on the fifth floor."

They took their leave. Windy and Drew went off to wherever skirts go to freshen up. Ray and I watched the dining hall empty and the staff begin a clearing up clatter.

"How the hell did you get roped into this?" I asked Ray.

"Windy asked Drew. Drew asked me," he said.

"Did Drew know I knew you?"

"Not that I know of."

"Did Windy?"

"Not that I know of."

"Did you tell them?"

"God no. I wouldn't dare. My uncle wants what you're doing kept way under the table," Ray said.

"Why you?"

Ray shrugged. "My guess is that Drew knows my uncle gives a lot of money to this bunch."

"And Drew knew Victoria."

"And she knew my uncle, and my uncle knew me."

"So, you didn't know Drew before?"

"First time I've ever clapped orbs on the skirt is tonight."

I kind of weighed the two of us, neither on the top rung of our world, and the two women.

"They must have really wanted to come to this gala," I said.

"Hey, they're women. They saw a chance to dress up," Ray said.

Yeah, I thought, *that and be followed around by two chumps*. But, as they walked back to us, I had to admit they were both good to look at. Drew in black, with a lot of shoulder and showy splatter of oranges and reds across her bust. Windy in clingy blues and a long rope of pearls. Both wore glittery diamond brain binders.

"Always the last one to leave, Gambler," Windy accused, moving up next to me.

Drew shuffled a quick Charleston move. "Rumor has it there's a dance going on. You boys wanna come?"

We offered our arms to the two women and walked them out. The last guests to leave the room.

Out of the doors, into the foyer, and the night spun out of control. For among the scatter of couches, there sat Poul, my Swedish sailor. My possible killer.

"Give me a few minutes," I said to Windy. I watched her walk away with Drew and Ray. She kept glancing over her shoulder at me. I waited. When the three of them turned into the room with the music booming, I went over to the sailor.

"Poul. It's Poul, isn't it?"

He took a moment to recognize me.

"The bootlegger, *ja*?"

"Yes." I sat by him. "I like your—what do you call them—your dress blues."

Dark navy blue. Brightly polished gold, braided rope at his shoulder.

"You brought me liquor," he said. "Lousy stuff. Most of it."

"Figured you could use it to clean your instruments."

"All it's good for." He made a face, then went on in that sing-song. "You got more of that good stuff?"

"Maybe I know a guy. Won't be a Christmas present, though. Three bucks each. Maybe four." I said, stringing him along.

Poul shrugged.

"Give me a couple of days," I said.

"I wait."

"You here for the dance?"

"*Ja. Ja.* I dance."

"I'm surprised, Poul." Kind of worried, too.

His eyes opened wider. "Why that?"

"Almost everyone came with someone. Not many women to dance with."

My Swedish sailor took a minute to sort through my American.

"Oh, *ja*. What you mean, I get. I come with someone. She go somewhere to put on lipstick."

"I see." More than I wanted to see. And I didn't have Bobbie Lee here to run interference. "Where do they go to do things like that? An age-old mystery, I suspect."

Christ, when did I begin to talk like Windy?

Poul had to sort through that too. When he did, he chuckled.

"Mystery for sure," he agreed.

"You coming?" I looked up to see Windy standing over me.

"Shall with your goat feet dance the antic hay," she continued. "With me. God help us all.

"Shakespeare?" I asked.

She shook her head. "The first part of it is Marlowe."

Whoever the hell that was.

"I know you," Poul said, looking up at her. Then he turned to me, eyes wide with wonder. "You got her? The one in the picture. The painting?"

"You know her from a painting?" Struck me like a thump in my chest.

"She looks like a painting I saw."

I shot a quick look at Windy's startled eyes.

"Where did you see this painting?" I asked Poul.

"Someone's house. Something is wrong?"

We were too obvious, I guessed.

"No. No. Was that someone named Mrs. Yeats?" I asked him, trying to make it as calm as I could. "Victoria Yeats?"

"Vickie, *ja*. Her name is, I think." His eyes went to Windy. "Pretty girl in painting. You are the painting, I think."

Windy just gawked.

"That means you've visited her at her house." A thought said out loud more than a question.

"Two times, I have. Maybe three," Poul said. He looked at us as we looked at him. "Did I do wrong?"

I didn't figure this to be the time to let him in on what we feared. Or of anything else.

"Nothing wrong, Poul," I said. "We're just surprised that you and I know the same people."

He got pouty. "It's, how you say, it's okay for American girl to like Swedish man."

"Sure it is, Poul." I rose to take Windy's hand.

"You're a lucky man, bootlegger."

"Why is that?"

"I've seen the painting," he said. "Don't forget me. Real stuff this time."

"Real stuff," I assured him.

It took effort not to look back at the Swede and to make it a stroll instead of a march toward the swing music. And to leave him to go home with some woman.

"What happened to Drew?" I managed a smile when I said it. In case he was still looking.

"She ducked as soon as she spotted the sailor. She didn't want to be anywhere near the man."

"Scared?"

"Even if she is not harmed, her heart may fail her in so much and so many horrors," Windy quoted in her theater voice and waited for me to respond, mischief in her eyes.

I held up my hands in surrender. "I'm not asking."

"Bram Stoker."

I had no idea who Mr. or Mrs. Stoker was, so I just kept walking toward the music.

Drew propped herself against the wall just inside the double doors. Like a dishrag hung on a peg. Ray hovered protectively before her. When her downcast eyes saw my shoes, she lifted them, pleading.

"I want to go home," she said.

Ray considered her for a moment.

"Because of the sailor?" he asked. "We won't let anyone hurt you, Drew."

"Mister Colleta, I don't want to be in the same building with that man." She slumped her shoulders even more.

I glanced at Windy. She jerked her own shoulders and nodded her head vaguely toward the street.

We piled in the Studebaker. Poul got left alone with whatever skirt took him to the dance.

CHRISTMAS PRESENTS

Windy pranced and danced a kind of Charleston shuffle up to dead Victoria's digs. Couldn't figure why she was so happy. I drug along behind, trying to see over our bundle of winter coats. A chump stomping after a skirt, just as predicted. Still, she was pleasant to watch.

By the time I got the coats on the rack, Windy had cranked up the Victrola. Rolling sax rifts, with brass and licorice sticks suiting her moves as she danced before the turntable.

"You stir up a fire. There's wood out on the back porch," she said over her shoulder. "I'll put on some coffee."

I was puffing on the bit of smoke I'd coaxed from the sticks when she brought me a steaming mug.

She stood over me and sipped her coffee as I worked the fire higher. The bank of ashes along the back helped throw out the heat from it.

As my knees popped and cracked getting up from the floor, Windy put her empty cup on the mantle.

"I have something for you." Windy reached next to the cup for a large book with a dull red cover.

I took it and gave it a heft. "Damn thing's heavier than my little sister."

"Like you ever had a sister." She smiled. "And that book has everything Shakespeare ever wrote. Read the introductions first. It'll make things easier."

"Thank you, Windy. I didn't bring your present. I'm sorry." I lied. Getting one for her had not even entered my mind.

"For it is in the giving that we receive," she said.

I gave the heavy book another heft. "More Shakespeare?"

"St. Francis of Assisi."

Windy stepped close to me and reached to pull loose the knot of my bowtie. Fingers rose to unbutton the top button of my shirt.

"There. Now you look like you're ready for business."

I took that as an invitation and closed the distance between us.

"Well, I never..." Windy looked up at me, fully expecting my hesitation. She got it.

She took the book from me, put it on the coffee table, and gave a silvery laugh.

"...I never, Gambler, never thought I'd see you ever make a move on me."

My hands came up and took hold of her face. The kiss was long. Windy's tongue fenced at my lips and mouth. Her leg pushed between mine, and she pressed her body onto me. Pressed some places more than others.

"About time," she said.

Then her hands came up my chest and her fingers curled under my collar. With strength beyond what I believed she contained, those hands ripped down.

Shirt buttons flew free, clattering here and there across the room.

Her arms snaked under my torn shirt to pull herself against me.

I pushed her back. It was my turn, damn it. I hooked fingers under the shoulder straps of her gown.

She made a quick intake of breath. Didn't need to worry. I knew better than to be ripping her clothes apart. I pulled the straps down from her shoulders and caused the gown's throat to press tight across her chest. Slower, I drew down the fabric. Her tiny breasts sprung free from the thing. I took the time to admire them.

Windy let me have that time. Then she giggled and turned, slumping her shoulders, showing the buttons down her back.

I did not rip them. When they were unbuttoned, the gown fell to the floor.

She turned and let out a scream. A feral cat scream. Her full lips parted. Those tiny teeth seized a wad of skin on my collar bone.

I screamed then. And maybe I screamed like a little girl.

Windy's full fury broke loose. Kissing and clawing. Buffeting and biting. She wrestled me more than anything. The couch. The coffee table. The floor where Victoria died. And too much of it was pain.

She ruined it. When I went after her more in anger than lust. Bent her over the table and pinned her down with a hand between her shoulder blades. She ruined it. Her startled eyes closed, and Windy smiled. She smiled again when I spent and collapsed on top of her.

Not too much later, Windy sat naked on the edge of the couch. She slouched back and stretched those milk-fleshed legs out before her and watched me dress.

"I liked it when you fought me," she said.

Putting on clothes had its puzzles. No buttons for the shirt. I felt it sticking to my back. It was a bloody, clawed up mess. Stepping into and pulling up those roomy slacks was a clown act. Especially under Windy's gaze.

She had the good grace not to laugh.

"We got him, Gambler."

"Got him?"

"Dead to rights. He knew Victoria. He'd been to this house."

I reached up to press gently at my swollen lower lip. Swollen where she'd bit it at some point.

"Maybe," I said.

"What more do you want?"

A confession might be nice. Him even looking guilty might be nice. I stayed silent.

Windy put her feet on the coffee table. Her toes stretched out to touch the big book.

"Don't forget your Christmas present."

My eyes went down from her green-eyed gaze, along her flawless torso, down those sculpted legs, to her perfect little toes.

"There are Christmas presents, and there are Christmas presents, Windy."

She laughed a quiet woman's laugh.

Grabbing the book, I went out into the cold and headed home.

"What in unholy hell happened to you?" Bobbie Lee said. He waited, alone in the room. The game over, everyone else had gone.

My lip was puffed up. My shirt open, without its buttons. The two half circles of teeth marks showed, looking like little blood blisters, a growing purple bruise spreading out from them. I never did get the jacket on, and God knows what happened to the damned bowtie.

I grimaced and pulled the back of the shirt from where it stuck to the clawed skin of my back.

"Leave off. I don't want to talk about it."

"Sorry, Conner. Just wondered what the other guy looked like."

"Like it never happened," I groused.

"Good in the clinches, huh?"

"I don't want to talk about it."

"Here's tonight's rake." Bobbie Lee gestured at the two stacks of greenbacks on the table beside him. Our stack wasn't as tall as the other one.

"What did we get?" I asked without really interested. Not that night.

"A hundred and ninety-eight bucks after the split."

"Damn." Not too shabby. "I see everybody got paid."

Bobbie Lee nodded.

"I'm going to bed. Lock up, will you?"

He nodded again.

I flopped into bed. Thought, to hell with blood-spotted sheets. But I didn't want to sleep. I wanted to think things out. About Victoria. I wanted to decide about Poul, the Merchant Marine doctor. I wanted to drive out the memory of naked Windy and the feel of her body thrashing me. The bitten lip. The teeth marks on my chest. The clawed back. Men are tom cats on a fence.

So, of course, I dumped into a deep well of sleep in seconds.

Bobbie Lee and Joe woke me as they puttered around in the front room. I ignored them and headed for a warm bath. The water didn't sting if my back was under it. I was laying on my side, facing the wall, when Jenny came in.

"Wait a second. I'll grab some clothes," I said over my shoulder.

"I've seen it before. Sit up." Jenny produced a bottle of gin and rummaged around for a couple of wash cloths.

She spilled some gin on one of the cloths, grabbed my chin in a hand, and dabbed at my swollen lip.

"Ouch."

"Real hellion, that girl," she said. "Why did she bust your lip?"

The gin, the smell of my bar soap, and her perfume clashed in the air.

"How do you know she busted my lip?"

"Oh, I don't know. The claw marks on your back. A complete set of teeth marks there." She poked my bruised chest.

"Ouch. She didn't bust it. She bit it."

Jenny swabbed the marks, too, though the skin wasn't broken there.

"Lean forward," she ordered.

I hissed like that tom cat. "Damn. That stings."

"Good."

"Good?"

"Yeah. Tangle with a baby tiger, you're due a bit of pain." Jenny laughed. "You know, Paddy, I think I might be a touch jealous."

I looked up into her eyes as she pondered me.

"I may have learned my lesson. You may not have much to be jealous of."

That started to be a bit of flirt but, as I said it, I realized it was true.

"First, I may hope you have. And second, I may hope I don't."

I smiled. It hurt.

"It wasn't a punching match, Jenny. Didn't leave a mark on her," I said. Though there might have been some bruises on her knees. Jenny just looked at me. "I thought I needed to say that."

She stood. "Maybe you should have. Don't spend all day in here." With that, she left.

I stared after her. I had never understood women. And I understood them even less as I sat there in bath water going colder by the minute.

Somebody was cooking when I came out. Beef and onions being fried. Rice being boiled. Had to be Mai. Jenny sat at the poker table and practiced her flourishes. Joe fiddled at the chessboard. Bobbie Lee slouched on the couch and thumbed through my Shakespeare book.

He caught me eyeing him.

"This thing weighs more than I do," he said, closing it. "Been book shopping?"

I shook my head. "Christmas present."

"Did you learn anything last night? Other than the obvious, I mean."

"What's the obvious lesson, Bobbie Lee?"

"Don't get into fights unless you know you can win, I think."

I laughed. "Next time I will, I promise."

He handed me my book. I sat in the chair across from him. Made my back sting.

Jenny came over to sit by Bobbie Lee.

"Well, did you ask different questions last night?" She asked.

"Didn't even have to. Not really," I said. "Found out that my sailor knew the murdered woman. Had even been to her house. At least twice."

"Once to kill her, you think?" Bobbie Lee asked.

I shrugged. "Well, he didn't come out and say so."

"Well, he wouldn't, would he," he said. "Do you think he did it?"

"Looking him in the eye—no, I didn't. He didn't appear like that." I shook my head again.

"He could have, though," Jenny said.

"Windy thinks so," I said.

"But you don't." She arched an eyebrow.

"Doesn't matter. Not right now anyway. I'm gonna work on the fool, Harold, first."

"Why him?" Bobbie Lee asked.

"Because he's easier to get to. And I'm needing your help."

"I know that look, Bobbie Lee. Watch out," Jenny warned.

"What? I'm gonna take him drinking. That's all. Simple."

"Wait for it," Jenny told him.

"And while I'm doing that, I want you in his house. Gotta tool kit?"

Tool kit, in our world, meant lock pick tools.

Bobbie Lee waited to erase the surprise from his face before he replied.

"I can get one."

"No jimmy. No crowbar. I don't want him to know you were there."

He waved his hand dismissively. "No jimmy. No crowbar. No problem."

"Yeah, no problem at all. Not one." Jenny showed her doubt.

"He's good, Jenny. Steal the boots off a cowboy without taking his dogs from his stirrups."

"What's he going to steal?" Jenny asked.

"Not a thing. I want him to look for poisons."

"When?" Bobbie Lee asked.

"Friday." I wanted my back to heal some.

Jenny leaned forward. "I trust you'll be asking different questions this time. Like we talked about."

"I think I'll just have to ask one question."

"What's that?" she asked.

"Tell me about Victoria."

"Just get him talking then?"

"Might work."

"Ha," Bobbie Lee said. "I don't think that'll get him to confess to killing her."

"He's hoping he might mess up," Jenny said.

"I'm hoping he might mess up." I wanted that so bad I just had to repeat it.

"It'll be nice to have you here tonight. Like old times." Jenny smiled.

"What do you mean? I only missed last night," I said in my own defense.

"And Saturday," Bobbie Lee said, happy to remind me.

"And two days last week," Jenny added.

"Okay. Okay. Any word on who we got coming tonight?"

"That brush over at the train station said a couple of guys off the five o'clock from N'orleans," Bobbie Lee said.

"Yuli thinks some jobbers from Fort Crockett are looking for a game," Jenny said.

"Army?"

"No. Contractors. Suppliers, he thinks," Jenny said. "They might be rounders."

She rapped the wooden edge of the coffee table for luck. Rounders hunt for a good, long game. They'd be good for us and our rake.

Mai called out that it was time to eat. We'd just finished when the marks started showing up.

Gray day. A chill wind drove ugly, low clouds south into the Gulf. Fitful spits of rain stung at the Island every few moments.

"Great day you picked," Bobbie Lee said.

"Isn't it, though?"

He stepped out of the rumbling Studebaker and pulled his coat tight around his throat. He pointed his gloved hand. "I'll be up under that tree. Ought to be able to see you drive by."

"Sorry you didn't bring a hat?" I asked him.

"Just be in the way."

"I'll try to keep ol' Harold drinking for about an hour. Don't be slow," I warned.

"That's if you can pry him out of his house at all," Bobbie Lee said.

"If not, I'll come get you."

He flashed me a grimace and shut the car door.

I rounded the block so the Studebaker would face the cross street where Bobbie Lee waited to watch for us to leave. If we left.

The car that guarded Victoria's house was not parked down the way. I wondered what happened to my cannon-toting thug. Maybe the weather caused him to stay home.

I put it out of my mind, and wondered, instead, why it took more effort to park the car than it should have. More effort to just walk up to Harold's door. Like my body didn't really want to make this trip. I did not want to make this trip.

Harold seemed both angry and puzzled on opening the door.

"Afternoon. Remember me?" I asked. He had a hard time looking me in the eye.

"Yeah."

"Uh, listen, you want to go grab a drink?"

"What?"

"I wanted to get out of the house. Grab a drink or two. Wanta come? I'm buying."

"Why me?"

"Why not? You're the only man I know in town." I said, thinking on the fly.

He considered me a minute. "You got family though. Right?"

"Tired of them. Baptists. You know?" Why not, I thought. A make-believe family's got a right to be Baptist. "Come on. It's just a drink. I'm buying."

"Where would you go?"

"I was hoping you'd have an idea. Don't know the town very much."

Harold looked this way and that, as if deciding.

"You're buying?"

"Yep."

"Let me get a coat." He closed the door in my face. A moment later he was buttoned up and on the way to my car.

He pointed the way to a neighborhood store around the block from Broadway. Just like Joe said, the back of the store had been given over to three pool tables. A row of slots lined the back wall.

Some old coot fed pennies into one of them.

The man I took for the store owner eyed us when we came in. He gave Harold a nod. One of recognition, not one of welcome, I thought.

"We're gonna play some pool," Harold said to the man. His wet shoes made dark spots on the worn wood floor as they slapped a trail toward the pool tables.

I made to follow, but the owner stepped in front of me.

"The tables are free if you're drinking," he said. An over-stuffed man, about two inches taller than me, and in shirt sleeves. Bad teeth and in need of a shave.

"Let me guess. My friend drinks beer."

"A pail," he assured me.

For some reason, I doubted my friend Harold shelled out that much—ever. I also remembered what Joe said about the man's beer.

"Get him his pail, I guess," I said. "You got anything harder? Anything that won't make me go blind?"

The man crossed his arms. "Got some rum. Straight off the boat from Havana."

"Set it up."

"Be a dollar and four bits."

Steep, but I figured sometimes a man had to pay to play. I fished out the coins, then followed Harold's wet footprints. Reminded myself that the bastard may have murdered Victoria.

Pool balls already clacked around the table, pushed by his hands. The sound echoed off the walls. Stale cigar smoke, sour beer, spilled liquor, old paint, and man-sweat haunted the place like invisible customers. That one guy, hunched over a penny slot, kept pulling on its arm. He didn't show any notice of us.

The owner came over, placed Harold's frothy pail on a stool, and pushed a tumbler of brown liquid into my hand. His eyes never met mine.

"Sing out if you want more," he said as he stalked out of the room.

Pegs set in the wall had stoneware mugs dangling from them.

Harold grabbed one and dipped into his pail. A good amount of the beer I paid for dripped to the floor as he gulped a mouthful.

"You play?" Harold asked. He put his mug on a stool, already ring-stained countless times. And grabbed a cue stick off the rack.

"Nope."

He put the stick on the billiards table and rolled it back and forth. To appraise it, I guessed.

"You sure? I'll be easy on you."

I shook my head and sipped my drink. Harsh on the throat, but not too bad.

Harold shrugged, picked up the stick, and started in on the white ball. Knocking it into first one red ball, then another. I stopped paying much attention to it.

"How's your father?" I asked.

Stopped him in mid-shot. He looked up at me. The glare of a cur dog straddling a fresh kill. He looked back down, made his shot. It scattered red balls all over the table.

"In the hospital. Dead by Christmas, the way I hear it," he said.

"I'm sorry to hear that."

"Puh, he wasn't much of a pa anyway."

Harold poked the cue ball with the end of his stick. Harder than necessary, by my reckoning. The balls clacked and thumped, here, there, and everywhere.

I had a thought then and went all cold inside. What about his mom? Did he even have one? Christ, she might be in the house when Bobbie Lee broke in. I tried to remember if Windy told me one way or the other. Couldn't.

"I hope your mom's doing okay with it all?" I ventured.

He shot me a jaundiced look.

"The consumption got her when I was little."

"Sorry."

"Barely remember the bitch."

Well, aren't you a delight, I thought.

A stranger interrupted the conversation. I was grateful. A tall gawk of a man, whose skinny head sat on top of a long neck that was mostly Adam's apple. Straw hat set back over a skull of lank, blond curls. Cheap suit. Flashy ring on a long-fingered hand.

"You want a go. Quarter a game?" the man asked. He had hustler written all over him.

Harold must have figured it, too.

"Nah. I'm done." He put his stick back in the rack. He looked back at me. "I want what you're drinking."

Sounded like a good idea to me. I shrugged. "Sure."

What went for a bar in this stinky room was a box of rough-hewn lumber. Pine and obviously handmade. Harold went up to it and bent over to lean on his elbows. Not much of a lean. He wasn't all that tall. I gave the wood a couple of raps, like I was knocking on a door.

The owner poked his face around the door. I pointed to my glass. "Two more of these, please."

The man gave me and Harold a look-over and gave a smirk.

While the man watched, Harold took his drink and gave it a thoughtful sip. The face he made was priceless. He let out a breath, like the rum punched him in the gut. I bit my lip, hoping to keep the grin off my face.

"Damn," Harold said. Almost a whisper.

"The second drink's easier," I said.

He swallowed, then snapped. "I know, dammit."

More breath than voice still, I thought.

"Tell me about Victoria?" I asked after he downed a third sip. "I know she was special to you."

"Yeah? How the hell would you know that?"

"Windy mentioned it."

"Windy mentions too much."

I held up a hand. "Meant no offense. Just talking."

"Seems like you'd know her well enough." He made another sip. "You're her brother-in-law after all."

Was I that? Brother-in-law? I'd told so many lies to this fool I couldn't sort them out. What had I told him? Maybe it was the rum.

"Remember, Harold, I don't live in town. Victoria came to a couple of Christmas dinners with us. She had me to the wedding. Her husband talked a little about her in letters. That's really it."

He looked at me a couple of seconds, expression unreadable.

"I liked her a lot. She liked me," he said.

"Tell me."

"She was nice. I'd go over to see her. She'd make me tea. Cookies."

"Yeah?"

"Cookies were crap."

"Not much of a cook, huh?"

"Nah. Not much. But she made 'em up. Brought 'em out."

"Nice gesture."

"It was. Made me feel good. I brought her stuff."

"What did you bring her?" I asked.

"Little stuff. I bought her a fountain pen once. A music box."

There was a music box in those things Windy gathered. She mentioned it, I think. Didn't say where it came from.

"Sweet, man. She must have liked that."

"She did." Harold answered me, then met my gaze. He didn't do that a whole lot. "We had plans, you know. Or, we did until that rich bastard turned her head."

"Turned her head?"

"Fancy clothes. Fancy cars. All that uptown crap. You know, turned her head." Harold took a sip. Hardly a grimace out of him that time. "Just stole her away."

"Must have been hard on you," I said.

"Hell with it. I gotta unload some of that piss water beer," he said, pointing over his shoulder.

A door in the wall that needed more paint than the rest of the room, had a weathered sign on it. Toilet. He stomped off to it.

I heard a quiet chuckle. The owner came around the corner. No smile on his face. Maybe the man didn't remember how.

"You know, there's not a skirt this side of town that hadn't loved him once. At least according to him. Every damn one of them got stolen from him. According to him." the man said.

"I guess, according to him, I should be impressed."

"You want another one?" He nodded toward my nearly empty glass.

I shook my head. "Maybe if Harold wants another."

He chuckled again. A phlegmy rumble. "If I pour him one, and he downs it, it's on the house."

Harold came back and put his elbows back on the bar. He didn't say anything, and he didn't look at me. Instead, one of his hands kept twisting his half-filled glass round and round.

I looked at him. Grimy finger nails. Tea-colored skin. Pasty, brown hair. He looked like he needed a bath.

"What?" he barked and gave me a bit of a glance.

"Nothing. Thinking about Victoria, I guess," I said. "Sounds like you missed her."

"Yeah. No. No, I don't. I took her..." he paused a couple of seconds. "I tucked my memories of her down deep. Keep her alive, in a way."

"I figure she's sittin' up in heaven smiling about that, Harold."

He snorted a laugh. "My old bastard father assured me that loose women always ended up in hell."

"Women like Victoria?" I asked.

"She was your sister-in-law. Did you think that?" Again he looked me in the eye.

"Not really."

"She got her head turned."

The crumb never did get that second rum.

MRS. COLLETA

"You look good, darlin'," Bobbie Lee told Mai.

She did too as she leaned against the counter in a clinging, long, Anna May Wong dress of a shiny blue fabric, trimmed at the throat and shoulders in gold needlework.

"Box that stuff up and put it on the shelf, Bobbie Lee. You broke into that house in broad daylight." Pure fiery anger shot from her dark, almond-shaped eyes. Cupid bow lips pouted.

Bobbie Lee pointed a finger at me.

"He made me," he teased.

"And you…" she started, giving me that gaze.

I held up placating hands. "It needed doing, Mai."

"For what? I don't see a pile of diamonds or stacks of gold bricks," she said.

"I had to find some things out." I crossed my arms.

"So you sent my Bobbie Lee into a house, in the rain, in daylight." She turned to Bobbie Lee. "And what did you find in there?"

He looked at me. I gave a nod before he answered her.

"Some poisons," he said. "And some chloroform, of all things."

Mai laughed. "That'd make things easier for some guys I know."

"Yeah," Bobbie Lee agreed. "That slagheap would probably find knockin' them out the only hope he had."

I would have agreed as well, but Joe stuck his head into the kitchen.

"You're needed," he told me.

When I got out front, I found the game stalled, and a big load of silence. Except for the hiss of the space heater.

Four players, all in their shirtsleeves. Two round-faced business-men, each with a small stack of chips before them. One chiseled stick of a man, propped on top of a big pile of chips, smirked. The fourth man, wiry hair askew, and ruddy face scowling, had locked eyes with Jenny. No chips laid in front of him. Her face placid, except for the start of a smile at the corners of her mouth.

I guess I needed a reminder that I was, after all, the owner of a poker game.

"Problem?" I asked.

The fourth man looked up at me. He seemed surprised at what he saw.

"You're the boss?"

"Yep. Strange, isn't it?"

"Okay, youngster. The pretty lady here won't honor my chit."

I glanced at Jenny. She kept a calm gaze at the man, though I might have seen the slight upturn on her lips go up just a little more.

"That's because I told her not to."

"My money's good."

"Doesn't look like you have any money."

"Soon as the banks open…"

"Next game's Tuesday. Come back then," I said.

"I got a good hand. Jesus, man."

"No chits. No checks. No IOUs. House rules."

"Can I get one of the players to back me?" the mark asked.

"As long as they know that we're not a collection outfit." I looked each player in the eye when I said it. "Back the man and you're on your own."

I heard later that one of the other players took the man's IOU. Three queens always beats three tens though. But I wasn't there to care, because of a knock on the door.

I listened but could not make out the rumble of Dutch's voice. He came around the oriental screen.

"Somebody wants to see Mr. Miles," he said.

"Ask them in."

"They won't come." he answered with a shrug.

A woman stood on my stoop. Tall. Brunette. Late thirties, early forties. Expensive, fur-lined coat. An unadorned, wool cloche hat. Gloves.

Behind her stood Ray Colleta, wide-eyed. Maybe even a bit fearful. His fedora didn't hide any of that. His head seemed hunched down into his black flogger.

"I'm Conner Miles."

"You will come with me," she said. Queen-like, I thought. She turned and started toward the Cadillac V-63 parked on the street. A long, swooping thing, shiny even in the dark.

"Why?" I asked.

She turned on her heel. "Because I said to."

Ray grimaced and gestured at me to come. I didn't think he would have done that if the woman had been facing him.

She was nobody's moll. In fact, she looked more like my fifth grade history teacher. And like that teacher, she spoke like she never took no—or even, why—for an answer.

This thing had trap written all over it.

Among the choices I'd made in my life, there were rides to dodge and rides to go on. I figured this was one of the latter. I swallowed, grabbed my hat and coat, and followed.

The woman let herself into the front seat. Ray got behind the wheel. He pressed the ignition and the Cadillac's eight cylinders rumbled to life. Before he put it into gear, he turned to me in the back seat.

"Conner Miles," he started. "This is Mrs. Don Colleta…"

"Donatus. Mrs. Donatus Colleta." she corrected.

"Nice to meet you, ma'am," I said.

She did not answer me.

Ray wheeled down to Broadway, turned west, then north. Another quick two or three turns then into the driveway of a substantial, well-lit bungalow. Big columned porch. Gables, one over the porch, one behind it and over the main body of the house. There must have been second story rooms up there. A brick chimney rose over all, from the center of the left side of the house. Looked like every light in the place was on.

Mrs. Colleta got out, then bent to look at me through the window.

"Come on, then," she said. She walked to the steps.

I knew she expected me to come behind her. Ray shot me a grin as I got out of the car. He stayed where he sat.

As God is my witness, a Negro maid, in a severely starched, black-and-white uniform, stood stiff and prim, holding the door open for me. First time that ever happened to this dumb Paddy.

Just past her, Mrs. Colleta stood waiting. She regarded me with frank, dark eyes. She'd shed the coat and cloche. As she gazed, her hands peeled off the clingy, tan gloves.

"Why you?" she asked.

She didn't want an answer, but I speculated over why she wanted to know. Or even what she wanted to know.

"Ma'am?" I removed my fedora.

Mrs. Colleta turned. "She's back in the parlor."

Hat-in-hand, I followed like her pet puppy.

What she called a parlor was directly behind what I guessed would be the living room, though that looked like a parlor to me. Ornate, wooden furniture upholstered in striped horsehair. Coffee and end tables of matching wood supported pale, shaded lamps that dangled falls of crystals. A time-stained oil of an ancestor hung above a fireplace stacked with oak and ready to be lit.

She, whoever she was, sat bolt upright on one end of the couch. Certainly Italian, like Mrs. Colleta. Handsome enough, but not pretty. Bold nose, hooked. Skin a pale olive. No makeup. Long dress and long sweater of beige wool. No hat covering her crow-black hair. Empty expression. Dark eyes studied the carpet.

"Julia? This is the man my husband wants you to talk to. Are you all right with it?" Mrs. Colleta asked.

"Berries," Julia said after three seconds of hesitation. I counted them. She did not look up.

Mrs. Colleta turned those hard, dark eyes on me and filled them with warning.

"Carefully, Mr. Miles."

"Yes, ma'am."

I waited for her to leave the room and pull the door closed before I took a chair across from Julia. I heard her shoes clomp as she walked toward the front of the house. I wondered if she made more noise than necessary on purpose. Maybe to assure Julia she wasn't eavesdropping.

"My fault," Julia said.

"Sorry?"

"It's my fault."

"What is?"

"All of it. It's all my fault." For the first time, Julia looked at me.

"All of what?" I asked. "Can you tell me about it?"

"You some kind of hero? Out to rescue the princess?"

I had to smile at that thought. "Don't know if I could rescue a pebble from a puddle, but I'm here, and I want to know what's your fault. If it's your fault. What happened?"

"There's something stiff over in that decanter. Pour me one," she said.

"That's all right with Mrs. Colleta?"

"She brought it. Or her maid did."

Glittery cut-glass bottle. Glittery cut-glass, lowball glasses. I poured us each one. A generous pour.

The woman swallowed a nice size gulp and didn't make a face. Then she watched me until I took my own gulp. Top shelf stuff.

"Good. I don't drink alone," she said. Any innocence in her left.

"What's your fault, Julia?"

"All of it. Just like I said."

I set the glass down. "If you don't want to tell me…"

"No. Please stay. If Mr. Colleta wants this, I'd best do it."

That was probably true. I picked up my drink and sat back.

"What's your fault?" I repeated.

"Finding myself half-dressed and alone in a strange hotel bed this morning. With no real idea about why I woke up there."

"No idea? None?" I asked because of the look on her face. She held something back.

Julia glanced at the closed door before she answered.

"I know how. I know why," she said. "Like I told you, I did it to myself."

I smiled at her. "I really need to ask you that how and that why, but I'm afraid to."

"Don't want to upset the dumb broad?"

"Don't see any dumb broads in the room."

Another glance at the closed door.

"Nothing said goes out of here? Especially to Mrs. Colleta?"

"Nothing."

"Swear?"

"Swear."

She looked at me a moment.

"How? I marched right through the rear door of that hotel, arm-in-arm with a good-looking man. Why? I went there to have a good time."

"Did you? Have a good time, I mean?"

"Yeah. Maybe. I'm pretty sure…" She pondered on it. "I indulged. A lot."

Okay. A skirt out for a good time got a good time. I started to get the idea that Mrs. Colleta didn't get the entire playbill. And, I couldn't get why I was here.

My mamma always said I was dumber than a sack of seed corn. Then it hit me, just like that sack of corn.

"This sharpshooter that asked you out…?"

"Sharpshooter?"

"A man spends a lot of money and dances a lot. I'm guessing he asked you to go dancing first."

Julia flushed all the way up to her ears. She swallowed hard.

"He didn't ask me first or any other time. I asked him. God, I sound like such a quiff. Like I just give it up to anybody."

Probably not to just anybody, I figured. Anyway, what the hell. She was a grown girl.

"Tell me about the man?" I asked, afraid I already knew the answer.

"Great dancer, like you said. Blond. Looking all Brooksy in his uniform. God, what an accent…"

I let her go on with her praise song of the Swedish sailor, Poul Osten. Good ol' Poul. Charmed her. Used her. Left her. I never figured women out.

"He didn't do what you're thinking, Mr. Miles," she said. She must have read the expression on my face. "I did all of it. To myself. This is my fault."

"You've said that."

"It's true." She set her face in what looked like defiance.

"Maybe it's sort of his fault, too." I said. She started to speak, but I stopped her. "Do you want anything done about this?"

"If anything is to be done, it needs doing to me."

I got a weird impression that Miss Julia wanted a paddle applied repeatedly to her high society bottom. A job for the skirt's father, not a job for me, I decided.

I stood. "Appreciate you talking to me, ma'am."

"Just berries. A night in a hotel turned me from a cancelled stamp into a ma'am." She managed a big eye roll as she said it.

I guessed it just might have at that. Didn't say that out loud, though. Instead, I put my hat in my hands and left the room.

Mrs. Colleta saw me from her place in the living room and rose to come my way. A middle-aged couple sat on the couch, each holding a small glass of something pink. Julia's parents maybe.

She took my elbow and led me further toward the front door. Thought she was giving me the boot. Her over-the-shoulder glance showed she just wanted me beyond the couple's stares.

"Did she talk to you?" Mrs. Colleta asked.

"Yeah."

"You didn't upset her, did you? How is she?"

"Seemed okay, ma'am. More embarrassed than anything, I think."

"I should hope so," she said, then lowered her voice to a whisper. "Always her own worst enemy. She did tell you it was all her own doing, yes?"

I nodded.

She crossed her arms and that queen's voice returned.

"No matter that, I don't think a woman, any woman, should be treated like that. I'm sure you agree."

"Yes, ma'am," I said, knowing full well she wasn't asking me.

"I got the impression my husband thought you'd be the man who would do something about—about this thing."

Was that the impression Donny Colleta laid on his wife? I wondered what other impressions he'd left. The last I heard, the woman was never supposed to know my big feet muddied up the Galveston sidewalks. Now, he's having her invite me over. And me not yet beyond considering her the one that did for Victoria Yeats.

She waited for some response from me. It never came. She opened the door.

"Ray will get you home," she said.

"Ma'am." I held my fedora just over my head and made a bit of a bow.

She drew herself up. Almost seemed to fill the hallway, fierce and regal.

"Do something about it, Mr. Miles."

She wasn't leaving any choice. I wasn't sure I had one anyway. I donned the hat and walked into the cold night.

"Sorry, Miles. She didn't tell me anything."

That's all I could get out of Ray Colleta. He wouldn't look at me as I stepped out of the Cadillac and waited for a moment to give him a last chance. I got nothing.

Three men still faced Jenny when I went inside. That poor fool who tried to give me an IOU must have lost. He sat on the couch near the fireplace. He didn't seem to be suffering much. Mai had him drinking and smiling while she sat beside him.

Jenny gave me a wink but swept up the cards for some shuffles. I shot a quick nod toward Bobbie Lee and Joe as they sprawled in chairs by the chess game. The lounge chair across from Mai and the mark looked inviting. Soon enough, my hat and coat hung on the rack, and my backside warmed the horsehair cushions.

Mai turned to me. "Want a Scotch, Conner?"

"You're a jewel."

She made the offer to the mark, who nodded.

"Lost it, huh?" I asked him.

"Not my night, I guess."

"Not more than you can afford, I hope."

"Naw. I'm tapped tonight. But the bank's open tomorrow…" he said. "I'll be all right enough."

Wasn't sure I believed him. Not from the look on his face.

Mai brought the drinks. The mark tipped his up and drank it down. I lit a butt and split my time between the smoke and the Scotch.

Mai made a face at me, full of some kind of message, then her eyes rolled over to the mark. She did it again more intently.

I was supposed to do something.

"Hey, Mister. What's your name?" I asked the mark.

He gave it to me, but I didn't really need it and immediately forgot it.

"Well, sir." I fished out a twenty from my pocket. "Take this. My friend will drive you down to Post Office street. Better than sittin' here staring at the gas fire."

The mark frowned. "What's down there?"

"Good Scotch and obliging women."

"Too much like charity. Don't need any charity."

"Not charity. Christmas. Merry Christmas."

Bobbie Lee appeared at my shoulder, hand already out. I hauled out the keys and gave them over.

Five dollars for a top-shelf skirt. Five for a couple or three drinks. Five for a hire heap to take him anywhere on the Island—twice. And five to put in his pocket. A good deal. The mark took me up on it.

But I got the real prize. Big bright smiles from Jenny and Mai. Even earned a big red lipstick tattoo on my cheek from Mai.

"You're the last of the nice guys, Conner." Mai patted me on the shoulder, then went to offer more of my whiskey to the remaining players.

Only time in my life, up to then, I'd ever had a woman—two women—thank me for sending a man to a whorehouse.

Lot of first times tonight. I grabbed up my Shakespeare book from the coffee table and hunkered down in the chair. Ignored and glad of it.

Shakespeare wasn't one to make life easy on a poor lost soul the likes of me. Most of it went right on by me. So, I made bits of it into puzzles to figure out. That was fun, sort of, and sometimes I even came across a couple of things Windy quoted.

A Midsummer Night's Dream was what I finally picked to read front to back. It seemed easier to understand than the others. Fairytale or not.

Anyway, Titania, Queen of the Fairies, for some reason, reminded me of Jenny. I'd never tell her that, though. Of course, Titania got slipped a love potion and falls for some guy named Bottom that had the ears of a mule.

Didn't last more than ten minutes. Instead, my Irish green eyes drifted up off the pages to stare into the hissing blue methane flames of the space heater.

Poul. What to do about Poul? The heater glowed steady, but my brain boiled like my granny's stew. My ears stopped hearing the rumble and shuffle at Jenny's table. The smells of pine, cigar smoke, and liquor ebbed away to nothing. If I noticed Bobbie Lee coming back, I didn't remember it.

Sometime later, Jenny eased up next to me, then sat on the arm of my chair. She lit a cigarette and handed it to me.

"Anybody home?" she asked, lighting one of her own. The place echoed silent emptiness.

"Just the two of us, looks like."

Jenny rapped knuckles on the top of my head.

"I meant in there, silly."

"Hollow as a poor man's coin purse," I said.

"Oh, a late night poet." She chuckled deep and low. "I guess that Shakespeare book's rubbing off on you."

I grimaced. "Not that. Please, not that."

The hand that tapped me came up to move a stray strand of hair off my forehead.

"You don't want to tell me what's banging around in there, huh?" She asked.

I looked up at her, then over to the heater flames, then back at her.

"Here, a while back," I started. "Probably an hour or two before I met you, now that I think about it, Sam Maceo plopped a bit of his Sicilian wisdom on me. You know, when he gave me all this."

"Yeah, what was that?"

"Mr. Miles", he told me. "Time for you to stop sweating and start bossing. Or something like that."

"And? I know there's an 'and' coming."

"And, I think I'm in a spot where I've got to do some sweating."

Jenny arched her eyebrow, but I let her puzzle it out on her own.

"What kind of sweating are you going to do in weather like this?"

"You'd be surprised."

"I might be. If you told me about it. But I don't think you'll do that."

Well, of all the possible choices I'd thought I have to do, not one of them she'd have any business knowing. And, honestly, I wasn't sure I'd want her to know I was capable of. If I was capable of any of them.

"I won't."

"Nothing you want to sweat over, is it?"

I shook my head.

Jenny messed with my hair again. I liked her next to me. Her warmth. Her perfume. Her touch.

"Conner, what do you want?"

"For Christmas?"

"No. I mean for overall. For your life."

"What a question to ask."

"I want an answer to it, too."

Nothing really came up as I thought about it. Or even for the couple of seconds more that I pretended to think about it.

I put a hand on Jenny's crossed legs. "Lady, I might just have everything I want."

"You're impossible."

"Really, Jenny, I don't think about things like that. In this life, I get what I get, so I try to want what I get. I guess."

"A leaf in the river," Jenny said. "You know. Adrift."

"I guess. Maybe. What do *you* want? I mean, overall. And I want an answer, too," I teased.

She looked at nothing for a moment or two. "I want what all women want."

"And that is?"

"I want enough."

"What's enough, for God's sake?" I asked. "Lots of men, in this thing of ours, go around like there's never enough. Women, too, I'm thinking. How much is enough?"

"You know. Enough. Enough, so I have a roof, and warmth, and money in the bank. Enough, so I don't have any fool man bossing me around."

Jenny rapped knuckles into my chest. Not too hard.

"Now, darling, when was the last time I ever tried to boss you?"

"Yeah, when was that?" Jenny touched a finger to her chin as if she thought there was once. "Well, if I remember that day…"

"There wasn't one, and I got even money there will never be one."

Famous last words, I was thinking.

"Well, Paddy, as you drift through this night, and if you stumble over some enthusiasm, I may let you make a request. Long as it's a request, not a damned order."

Funny thing, enthusiasm. It can be found in the strangest places and the strangest times.

I stood, took her hand, and requested that she follow me.

ADRIFT

Dutch was a good kid. Big as a door. I didn't know anybody as quick to smile or as slow to anger. Of course, a man, or ten, trying to stand in his way would get washed away like a flash flood. But the grin wouldn't leave his face. He liked making money selling liquor, and didn't seem to mind towering over the marks he let into the house to play poker.

Figured he'd never get over that limp he got from the load of smuggled booze falling on his leg. It didn't seem to slow him up much.

I was glad to have him on my crew. Especially on that day.

"Who's the Laq fella?" Dutch asked as I inserted the over-sized skeleton key into the lock of the door of an abandoned warehouse.

"Can't you tell, Big Bit?" Bobbie Lee gave a smirk. "He's the keeper of the keys."

"The keys to this dung heap, Little Bit?" he returned.

Actually, Laq was a skinny, skittish little pencil pusher that helped herding up and driving out the Negro dockworkers on the piers. He could be downright helpful if I crossed his palm with a bit of money.

Crossing that palm got me a key and the address of the vacant warehouse it opened.

The entryway was dark despite the hazy sunshine outside. The several offices partitioned off on either side were as dark. But banks of grimy, high windows in the open area in the back gave us muted light.

The whole place smelled musty, with the tang of long dead vegetation. Dead rats too, if I tried hard. Didn't try too hard.

I turned to Dutch and Bobbie Lee. "Spread out. See if you can find something we can sit on."

"Where do you want them? If we can find anything?" Dutch asked.

"Right about here." I pointed down at my feet. "Where we can see."

He and Bobbie Lee wandered back toward the offices while I kicked around looking for, and hoping not to find, the source of the dead rat smell. The glamorous life of a gangster.

Quick enough, Bobbie Lee returned with a beat up milk crate that somehow kept a bit of the red paint that once covered it.

The throaty screech of furniture dragged across cement echoed the hollow warehouse. Scared the two of us. Both reached for pistols. But Dutch appeared, awkwardly hauling a rough plank bench behind him. Not a bench for sitting, for muddy boot tracks scaled the top of it. A bench for standing on.

He turned to grin at us, proud of his find. Bobbie Lee and I looked at him.

"Good, huh?" he asked, dropping his end of it with a bang.

I shrugged and nodded.

"Kinda dirty, ain't it?" Bobbie Lee commented.

"Don't worry, Little Bit, I'll fix it." Dutch started sweeping the crud off with bare hands.

I watched him foul up the already dirty floor. No possible way he'd get it clean enough. As boss of this raggedy outfit, I decided the rickety, red bottle crate would be mine to sit on.

Done, Dutch slapped dried mud from his hands. Left a brown cloud floating in the air.

"So, now what?" he asked as he plopped his clean pants onto the bench.

Bobbie Lee remained standing. "Yeah, so now that you've gathered us all here…"

"Okay," I said, then I told them.

I told them in detail. Enough details anyway. I kept it simple, telling them just what to do. No more. No less. Leaving me room to wiggle if I had to change things.

"Got it?" I asked. I looked both of them in the eyes until I got a nod from each. "Dutch, get that brandy in here. Bobbie Lee, you and I'll go to fetch Poul."

"What if he ain't there?" Bobbie Lee asked.

"Then we wait."

"If he don't want to come?"

"He asked for the brandy." I shrugged like it was a foregone conclusion. And I hoped that was true.

All I wanted was to get that Swede here and talking. He had something to answer for. Maybe a bunch of somethings. Somehow, I needed to get him here and get him flapping his mouth.

I'd started to sweat despite the chill. I also figured on more sweat work to come. Reminded me of what I'd told Jenny earlier.

"Ready?" I asked Bobbie Lee when we reached the street.

The breeze had picked up. If anything, the cloud cover had thickened.

"Loaded and cocked," he said. He always was, as near as I could figure.

I grinned. The wind stirred his blond curls. With his toothy smile, he still looked like a kid dressed up in his daddy's clothes.

"I'm ready. You bet on it," Dutch said. He carried the brandy crate like it was a box of chocolates.

"Grab yourself a patch of that filthy bench. We'll be back as soon as we can." I thumbed toward the warehouse. "Don't be cracking open any of the booze, huh."

"Not me." Dutch disappeared into the building.

I turned to Bobbie Lee. "Let's walk."

"Walk? There's a perfectly good car right there," he said, wide-eyed.

"Walk anyway," I said.

"Well, damn," he said, but we walked anyway.

Fetching Poul took a shout up the gangplank to the blond sailor on watch. A lot of blonds in Sweden, I figured. Moments later Poul bounced down from the ship, still buttoning his coat.

Bobbie Lee reached to pinch a bit of the dark blue fabric. "Geez, I want one. They did you good with that coat."

His envy sat plain on his face. I had to admit, that was one fine garment. Calf length. Shiny, large brass buttons. Brown lapels and collar. Pull that collar up and it kept the ears snug and warm. Heavy wool. Heaviest I'd ever seen.

"You have it?" Poul asked.

"I know where it is," I told him. "Just a short walk."

He said something that sounded like: "Are-day-tune-ja."

Earned him an arched eyebrow.

"Heavy? Much to carry when I come back?"

Carry back? I didn't know if poor old Poul would be coming back. And that sorry thought made me sick to my stomach.

All the clanging, rasping, thudding noises fell behind—ghost sounds of a haunted cathedral. Smudged, grayed buildings, mottled with a sea-stained blight, reduced the sounds to echo shadows. And their blackened windows stared down at me—the eye sockets of grave-robbed skulls.

Bobbie Lee? Poul? I didn't think they noticed. Too busy chattering about the glories of pre-prohibition liquor.

I pushed at the door of our skull of a warehouse. It opened like a swamp gator's maw at midnight. Like an invitation. Come on in, last of the nice guys...

Again, the sickly sweetness of dead rats.

Trusting, Poul plunged right in. Bobbie Lee followed and passed me a malicious grin on the way. Did I feel like a heel? No, I felt like chewed gum stuck on a dirty shoe. I went in anyway.

Dutch stood from his place on that dirty bench, the liquor crate at his feet.

He didn't wait.

Poul got close. That fist, the size of a ham, torpedoed into Poul's heavy coat.

He folded around it and dropped like a sack of laundry.

Ugly sucking sounds filled the empty air. Hurt me all the way to my teeth to listen to it. I looked at Bobbie Lee's grimace. He held his stomach as if he'd taken the punch himself. Mine didn't feel all that good either.

I pulled the empty crate up near Poul and squatted on it. He sucked air back into his lungs, or tried to, as I watched.

"What the...?" he tried. "Why?"

"That's from Julia's father."

"*Vem i helveta...?*" he managed. "Who in hell is...?"

"Julia? She's that skirt you slipped the Mickey Finn to. Remember? Right before you plowed her berry patch?"

Poul sorted through my English.

"*Nej.* No. No slipped," he rasped. "She asked for it."

"Jesus, man. No woman asks to be passed out before some bastard rapes her."

"No," he said again. "My opium. She asked for my opium."

"She asked for opium? You had opium?"

"*Ja. Ja.*" Poul reached into his coat with his free hand. The other still pressed his middle. He pulled out a vial of some milky liquid. "I always have. And she never *gick ut...* never passed out. Not 'til later."

Yep. Right there on the paper label. *Tinktur av Opium, 75%.*

"Not 'til later, huh?"

"*Ja.* Later she sleep."

Well, the little quiff. She told a bit of truth when she blamed herself.

Dutch stepped over in front of Poul.

"Okay," he said. "She asked for it. Okay. But when you got done with her you just threw on your clothes and left her there."

"No. No." Poul waved his hand and worked at sucking air into his lungs. "I wake her and wake her and wake her. She just pull blankets back on head. Go back to sleep.

"So she did pass out," I said.

"*Ja. Ja.* Later. Later..."

"When you were done, huh?" Dutch said. This time it was an accusation.

"Not like that." He sucked more air. "More true, she sleeped, slept, when she was done."

Now it was my turn to sort out what he said. I thought about the things Julia told me about that night. About the way she said them. About what Poul just said to me. The way he said what he said.

It began to feel like that night was really Julia's night. More her night than Poul's night. She had told me she had marched into that hotel's back door with—with—Poul. Maybe she led Poul into it. I'd figured the sailor had baited a trap and sprung it. That might not have been true.

And that left me nowhere.

I took off my fedora to fiddle with the brim a moment. Poul still labored for breath as he lay half-curled on the dirt of the floor. A lot of dust smudged his great wool coat.

Truth told, I felt sorry for the guy. Something I couldn't afford. Not on the chance this fool Paddy got convinced it was him that murdered Victoria Yeats.

But damn, the Swede's blue eyes looked up at me. Hurt. Wary. Betrayed.

Too soft. Too soft to say no to my boss. Too soft to say no to Colleta. Was I too soft period?

"Is your message delivered?" I asked Dutch, as if that was the reason he was in the room.

"You tell me," he said.

I tossed my head, looking toward the door.

"You sure?" he asked me and I nodded.

He stepped around to give Poul a final silent threat then left the room. Like I wanted him to.

Bobbie Lee kept his place and stayed silent. Like I wanted him to.

Poul watched Dutch leave. Propped on his elbow and holding his stomach, the poor fool looked young, even child-like. He was no child.

"Did Victoria Yeats want any of your opium?" I asked him.

"No," he answered. His sing-song gave the word two syllables. Maybe he still had trouble forcing sound from his lungs. "She never asked. Never knew I kept any."

He didn't sound like he lied. I propped my elbow on my knee, set my chin in my palm. We stared at each other, suspicious, hostile. Like new neighbors.

I listened to the sound of distant traffic, hollow and muted in the warehouse. Some rattletrap truck on the way to the piers.

"It's like this," I said to him. "Stay away from the free dances. Stay away from Galveston ladies. If you gotta, go to one of the houses up off Post Office Street. You won't be making any of their fathers angry."

Poul shifted. He noticed that I dropped my hand close to the pocket of my flogger. The pocket where my pistol was.

"I sit. I sit. Only that." He cringed as he sat up. Only that, like he said.

"You understand, right?"

Poul gave me a glance. "No dances. *Begripa*. I understand."

I stood without being sure he did understand. Because he remembered the brandy.

"*Kinjak? Konjakvin?* The brandy, *ja*." He pointed at the crate. "I have the money."

"Merry Christmas," I said as I looked down on him. I left him on the floor. Alive one more day.

————————⊰⋅⟐⋅⟐⟐⋅⋅⟐⟐⋅⊱————————

Bobbie Lee shook his head. Every time I looked at him on the drive back, he shook his head.

"What?" I asked.

"We should've left him there," he answered and shook his head again.

"We did leave him there."

"But he was still breathing."

"Can you say for certain he killed Victoria?"

"He might have. That's for certain." Bobbie Lee nodded.

"So we start killing everybody that might have done it. You know, just in case."

"Yeah. Just to be sure," Bobbie Lee said. A smirk. As if he was kidding.

But I knew he was only kidding if I was against it. I shot him what I wanted to be a withering look.

"Maybe tomorrow, you bloody-minded bushwhacker," I rumbled.

He laughed. "Maybe. Anyway, we got the Christmas party tonight."

"Aw, hell!" I had forgotten.

So Bobbie Lee got dropped off and I went hunting for a gift.

Not for Jenny, or Mai, or my crew. I'd taken care of them. I owed Windy a gift. Damn Shakespeare.

An hour-and-a-half, three cute salesgirls, and six bucks later, I knocked at Victoria's door with a gift-wrapped package held in front of me.

Windy's eyes widened when she recognized who stood at the door. Surprise, I guessed. But they dropped to the bright square I clutched close.

"Beware of Greeks bearing gifts," she said.

"Shakespeare?"

"Virgil, a Roman poet."

"I am slow of study," I quoted, remembering something I read in *A Midsummer Night's Dream*.

She laughed. "Well, blouse my bloomers. Look at you throwing Billy Shakespeare around my front porch. I am swept off my feet. Come in before more cold blows in."

The door squeezed me as she closed it quickly.

I didn't know why I'd brought Windy a gift. Did I owe anyone a Christmas gift if they gave me one first? But I wanted to see her. To look at her. Untamed brunette hair spilling to her shoulders. A trusting face that was angel and imp all at once. Wide green eyes. Cupid bow lips. Flawless, translucent skin. All set off by her cream-colored house dress, decorated with chocolate-colored lace with pearls beaded to it. She looked like dessert.

"You've changed things," I said when I could make myself look away from her.

"Didn't I though." Windy smiled. "Victoria liked the glitz and glow a bit too much. Tell me you agree."

Windy had ditched a good handful of Victoria's shiny metal pieces. Stark, towering lamps had been replaced by softer glass and crystal ones. She'd given a concession to the season with some porcelain baby dolls in Santa suits and a homey Christmas tree just a little taller than she was. But most prominent was the revealing poster-like portrait of a barely clad Windy surrounded by butterflies and ivy.

"So, your father couldn't find a place in the Opera House for that?" I pointed to the painting.

She laughed. "He probably could have but my mother thought it better somewhere other than on public display."

"I bet she did," I said. "Well, I'm glad it's back home at Victoria's."

"Not at Victoria's. At Windy's. This is my house now."

"It is?"

"Yes. Victoria left it to me. They read her will a couple of days ago."

"Nice," I said, but I remembered that shudder I felt sitting alone in this very room a while back. Victoria's ghost? Well, that chair was gone so maybe her ghost was as well.

"It is, isn't it?" Windy swanned over and looked at my package. "What's this?"

"Oh, yeah. Merry Christmas," I said.

Windy rolled her eyes. "I wonder what it could be."

Flat. Square. Thin. Roughly the size of a small tea tray.

"Hmm, what could it be?" I handed it over.

She tore into it. "My, it's recordings."

"Some opera, heavy on the Italian. And some blues, heavy on the Sax."

"Geraldine Farrar and Mary Lewis. My favorites." Her smile was a blessing, even though she breezed past the blues record. But she reached to kiss me on the mouth and that made it okay. "Thank you."

"Well, you're damn welcome," I said, breathless.

"I was about to make dinner for myself," she said. "Pork steak smothered in onions. A baked potato big enough to share. You'll stay, won't you?"

She didn't miss my hesitation.

"Oh, that's right. Gamblers work nights. I forgot."

"I'm sorry." I let her believe that. Easier than telling her I was going to a party I couldn't invite her to.

"Well, I'm keeping you long enough to have some coffee. Your poker players will have to wait." Her eyes dared me to say no. "Put on Geraldine will you? Be right back."

She padded off, barefooted, toward the back of the house. The floor had to be cold on those pretty feet but I talked myself out of offering to build a fire. I couldn't afford to get either of us too comfortable. Not that night.

The singer's voice trembled out of the Victrola's horn, full of the throaty overtones that I hated about opera. I knew who she was. She'd done several moving pictures but I'd never heard her before. I'd even seen one or two.

I promised myself I wouldn't offer any opinions on opera.

"Oh, good," she said, coming back with a couple of steaming mugs. "Over every mountain top lies peace. In every tree top you scarcely feel a breath of wind. *The Wanderer's Night Song*. And it's German, not Italian."

"Sorry," I said. A word I used a lot to Windy.

"Don't be, Gambler. It's one of my favorites. It goes on to say: 'Wait, you too will be at peace.' Only in German."

I smiled at her.

"Lookin' forward to it," I said. "Being at peace, I mean."

"Take your coffee," she ordered. "And you can sit down now."

I obeyed. Windy sat on the opposite end of the sofa and crossed her legs.

"So, you're not finding your life here on the Island very peaceful, are you?" Windy asked.

"Peaceful enough," I said. "There've been worse times now and then. Wilder."

She smiled. "Some man, Chesterton I think, said that the Irish are the men God made mad because all their wars are merry and all their songs are sad. Are your wars merry, Conner?"

"Wars?"

"Your struggles? Your work? The things you have to do?"

I didn't think Windy asked about my poker games. She was asking about finding out who killed Victoria. And maybe about doing something about it. In my mind, I saw the image of Poul sprawled on a warehouse floor. Then of Harold slumping over a dirty bar, telling me of all the women who loved him. I shook my head.

"No. Not very merry, Windy," I said. "And I haven't listened to a sad song recently."

She looked at me over the top of her coffee mug. "That's all you've got to say about it, huh?"

"Irish or not, my life is boring." That was a lie, but there was nothing about any of my wars or struggles I felt like bragging about.

"Gambler, I seriously doubt that," she said as the recording ended. "Let me try that other one. Do you want more coffee while I'm up?"

I shook my head again.

She changed the recordings out, gave the crank a few turns, sat the needle down, then returned to the couch. Mischief came into her eyes. She extended her leg to touch my calf with some pretty little toes.

"I'd lay a bet, Conner, that if you wanted to, you could stay awhile. If you wanted to."

I wanted to right then. Jesus, I wanted to.

"Sorry, Windy. I..."

"I know. You work nights."

A gangster's life is filled with lies.

A few minutes later I stood by the Studebaker, in the growing dusk, and stared at Victoria's house. No. It was Windy's house now. I remembered that strange feeling I had the first time I came here to sit on that chair and look down on the floor where Victoria died. To sense her ghost.

My aunt Gracie lived in a house with a ghost. Kitchen cabinets and drawers opened on their own. Once a drawer opened and a heavy fork was thrown across the room to clatter on the floor. Everyone was in the living room, and the back door was locked. Late in the night, when I visited, I listened to the ghost. It paced up and down the endless hallway, front to back, back to front. Floor boards creaked and squealed.

I never could understand how my aunt remained in that house. But she swore it was a friendly ghost.

As I watched, the porch light of Windy's house flickered. Twice. At me? Was Victoria's ghost friendly? I worried over Windy living there. And something nagged at me about the whole thing. Couldn't figure what.

RED STRING

"So what am I supposed to do with that?"

I plucked a chunk of Yuli's plum pudding from the debris field of cakes, cookies, cheeses, and breads. The remains of our Christmas buffet. But the chunk that quickly got popped in my mouth wasn't what I asked about. I asked about my new, second poker table. My Christmas gift from Rose Maceo.

"Put it to work. That's why he gave it to you," Jenny said.

"You think you can work two tables at once then?"

She made a wry face. "Of course not. We'll have to get someone."

"You know anybody?"

"Nope." Jenny shook her head, only half-attentive to me.

She lifted my present higher and admired it. An ermine hand warmer in which she had tucked her magic hands. She called it that. I thought it was called a muff. Didn't matter. Jenny seemed immensely pleased with it and I glowed.

"Like it?" I asked and nodded toward the fur.

Jenny purred and rubbed the ermine against her cheek, eyes closed, lips curled. "It's wonderful, Conner. I love it."

I couldn't make that throaty purr like she did. If I could've, I would've.

"I'm glad."

"What I got you was okay?" she asked, wide-eyed and tentative.

The three books she gave me laid stacked on my new table. I put my hand on them and grinned.

"Sherlock Holmes, huh?" I asked.

"Seemed to fit with trying to puzzle out stuff in your life and all," she said. "You don't like them?"

"No. I do. I can't wait to read them." I laughed.

It wasn't much of a laugh, but I meant what I said. Jenny didn't look convinced. She stared at me. That look of hers that tried to see deep into me.

"You've already puzzled it out, haven't you." she said. It wasn't a question.

Had I?

"What makes you think that?"

"Your ugly, Irish mug, Paddy. You have more tells than the sunrise."

Yeah. An easy read. And Jenny read me better than most. Anyway, did or didn't, I wanted to talk about something else.

"Gee, you think I'm ugly." I pouted.

"No, Conner. I don't," she whispered and brushed some finger-nails along my arm.

Along with the inner stir of Jenny's touch came a reminder of every-one else in the room. Even though no one paid any attention to us.

"Joe," I called.

He squatted against the stones of the hearth, a glass of Mai's concoction in a fist. No girl came with him to the party.

He looked up.

"Joe, you're my new dealer," I told him.

His mouth dropped open. "Why me?"

"Why not you?"

"I don't know nothing about dealing."

"Then maybe you should hire somebody that does to teach you." I turned to Jenny. "Can you have him ready by Christmas?"

"Don't worry, Joe. You were born to it," Jenny said with her break-heart smile.

I looked around my crew. Bobbie Lee on the chair. Mai in his lap, wearing shiny red silk. Dutch on the couch, his huge arm draped around a mousey brunette, whose hat pushed at her brow, and sloped down to her ears. Swarthy, piratical Yuli snuggled against a sweet, plump, ginger-haired flapper as the two crowded the couch with Dutch and his date. Dutch's girl watched me with the guilty eyes of a baby caught in the cookie jar, as if I'd up and shoot her. Yuli's dumpling stared, wide-eyed and eager. Like a virgin taking her first wrong turn.

Dutch and Yuli had plans for these girls. Those plans showed in their eyes. Joe leaned against the wall, pondering his new future.

"You men ready to dig into this?" I put my hand on the fat envelope that came with, and sat on, the new poker table.

That brought cheers. They figured it contained money. It did.

I went around to the other side of the table and started dealing out the money in stacks. One twenty dollar bill at a time into five equal stacks. Bobbie Lee, Joe, Dutch, Yuli, and me.

Three twenties were left over.

"So, what of these?" I asked them.

Bobbie Lee pointed at me. "They go to you. You're the boss."

"I might be. But we're together in this." An idea came to me, so I laid the three bills aside. "I'm a gambler. So let's gamble."

Jenny's chip tray sat in its place on the other table. I grabbed up a random fist full of them.

"All right. There's more than two and less than twenty. Pick a number."

Joe picked seven. Dutch twelve. Yuli four. Bobbie Lee nine. I slapped the chips down on the table but kept my hand over them.

"Wait," Bobbie Lee said. "What's your number?"

"Nope. I'm the dealer. You're the players." I removed my hand and counted. "Five. It's yours, Yuli."

The three bills went on a stack that I gathered up and gave to him. All the remaining stacks went into grateful hands, including mine.

"Now go on home. And don't spend all of it before daybreak," I said. "Oh, and Merry Christmas."

Mai gave me a big ol' hug on her way out. She and Bobbie Lee were the last ones out. Last except for Jenny and me.

Jenny had slid up to sit on the new table next to my pile of money.

She gathered it up, and handed it to me. I took it and scooched up next to her.

"Do you want a drink?" she asked.

"Naw." I shook my head. "You?"

"I'm good." She pulled her new muff from behind her and petted it. A wistful smile showed on her face.

"Jenny," I said. "I don't have it puzzled out, you know."

"Maybe you do and you just don't know it yet." She didn't look at me when she said it.

"Maybe."

"What's got a hold on you?"

"Choosing wrong."

That was the truth of it. If I got things wrong... The wrong person... Hell, there'd be blood on my hands, on my soul. I had to choose right. God damn Donny Colleta.

"Oh yeah, I've got something for you. Almost forgot." Jenny hopped off the table and went for her little spangled purse left stuffed on a shelf under the bar.

She came back with a bit of red string. "Hold out your hand."

I pushed out my left arm, making a dumb show of it. Jenny tied the string around my wrist with an intricate knot.

"What is it?"

"A piece of string," she teased, with a quirk of her lips.

I shot her a look.

"It's something my mother used to do for me. For days I was hurting or afraid. It wards off the evil eye."

"Woman's magic."

"Mother's magic," she countered. "Don't take it off. Ever. It can fall off on its own. Or disappear. That's all right. Don't take it off yourself."

I looked at it, turning the wrist back and forth. "Woman's magic."

"Mother's magic. I told you." She shrugged. "It will protect you."

"Protect me from what exactly?"

"From your choices."

Jenny helped clean up before she left. I was happy enough that she left. Clean house or not, I felt dirty. As dirty as that warehouse bench. Having the Swede roughed up did not sit well.

So I poured myself too much Irish whiskey, swallowed it down, and took myself to bed.

Good night's sleep. No Swedes, no creeps, and no murdered women tainted my dreams. I gave my whiskey the credit.

My morning bath wasn't all that bad either. At least as long as the water stayed warm. I even felt less dirty than I did last night. But when I'd toweled off and started to shave, I heard the clatter of pots and pans coming from the kitchen. My reflection in the mirror frowned back at me. Being alone with my morning coffee was what I'd looked forward to.

I found Jenny in the kitchen drawing water for our over-sized stovetop kettle.

"You're out and about, and clanking around early this morning," I said with no smile.

"Well, good morning to you to, Mr. Grump."

"No coffee?" I pointed at the kettle.

"No. Mai's coming over. She's making us tea."

"Why?"

"It's a mystery."

Not to her, I didn't think. Her mouth was quirked with mischief. The smile I knew stonewalled further discussion.

She put the kettle on the stove and stuck a match to light it. I pulled out a Fatima and lit it from that match.

"Where's mine?" she asked.

I put the cigarette in her lips, and fished out another for myself. Jenny struck another match for me.

"Go sit down while I tend the water. Do you want some toast, some bacon, or something?"

I patted my belly. "Nah, I'm good. Maybe later."

"Any later and you'll have to make it yourself," Jenny said to the back of my head as I went out to the front room and the fireplace.

Something was cooking beyond just the kettle. I just didn't know what. Yet. It took a while for the gas fire to heat the room.

A few minutes later, thumps sounded at the front door.

Mai kicked at the door with the toe of her shoe. She carried a sizeable straw basket. A checked cloth, like an Italian café's table-cloth, hid whatever it held. Behind her stood an old Asian woman. Older than Noah by the look of her.

I opened the door and reached to help Mai with the basket. She turned it out of my reach.

"No, no, Conner. This is for us women to do today," she said and pushed her way in. The old woman came behind her, bowing as she edged by me.

"Well, good morning then," I said.

"Good morning yourself." Mai wormed toward the couch, moving the basket to and fro to miss bumping into things. "Is Jenny here? She's supposed to be here."

"Kitchen. Boiling water, I think."

"Good. Just what we need." Mai set the basket on the floor, but it was the old woman that began to unpack it. "My *Da Yima* will make tea."

"Your what?"

"My great aunt. My grandmother's sister. Die-yee-mah."

"Die-yee-mah," I repeated, looking at the woman.

"We call her Ayi," she sounded: '*ah-yee.*'

"Ayi," I said and gave her a nod.

The old woman bowed to me. I bowed. She bowed.

"Sit, Conner. You'll kink something," Mai ordered.

Only after I sat did Ayi continue with the things in the basket. Some small, shallow bowls. A couple of containers with lids. A fragile looking tea pot. Something metal that looked like a tiny strainer. A white tray. All save for the strainer, made of a white ceramic with dark blue Chinese script glazed onto them.

Jenny came in with the steaming kettle and a cork hot pad I didn't know we had. She put them on the coffee table and greeted the two other women. She called Ayi by name.

Ayi threw a storm of nasal, discordant Chinese at Jenny. She arched an eyebrow at Mai.

"She says thank you for the water," Mai said.

Sounded like more than that. And a glance at Jenny's knowing smile, showed that to be so. I said nothing.

Ayi continued to fiddle with her tea set. After a few moments she poured some tea into one of the shallow bowls and held it up to me.

"Ching-zam-yong," she sounded.

"My *Di Yima* says for you to enjoy. Please take it with both hands." Mai looked at me. "Don't forget to smile."

I took it with both hands and a smile. "Thank you."

"*Shuh-shuh. Shuh-shuh* means thank you." Mai said.

I repeated that, or tried to. The two women exchanged a glance and giggled. The tea tasted all right—for tea. A grassy smell, watery, a touch bitter, and a little bit sweet.

"Sip. Don't guzzle," Mai warned. "It's impolite."

I thought I'd done that. My second go barely wet my lips. "What's impolite, young ladies, is not telling a person why he's being ambushed by a bunch of pretty women."

"Jenny told me it had to do with your choices." Mai shot a glance at Jenny. "Well, that's what she said. I didn't understand it."

I did. Maybe. Or thought I did, damn it. The red string tied around my wrist. Some of the color had bled during my bath, staining my wrist pink. My eyes glanced down.

Mai and her great aunt noticed. Ayi made another flurry of nasal Chinese, then made a quick gesture with her fingers. Like she warded against a hex or an evil eye of her own. Mai nodded sagely.

"*Shuh-shuh*, Mai," I said and sighed. They knew something about such strings. I was not about to pursue it.

A choice.

"All right, what's all this?" I looked at Jenny.

She gave me that mischief grin always meant to soften me up. "What? Do you feel invaded?"

"Bushwhacked more like. Why are y'all here?"

"I got them here to help you."

"Help me how?"

Jenny reached to touch my wrist. To touch that red string. "To help you with your choices."

"You and Mai still think Mrs. Colleta killed the Yeats woman." It was not a question.

"Anyway you, Irishman, still thinks she didn't," Jenny said. "Women can't do murder?"

"Do you do murder, Jenny? Or Mai? Or that old auntie of yours?"

"Mai told me she knew about what happened to her granny's husbands."

I almost choked. Those poor men, three of them if I remembered right, may have been poisoned.

"Are you okay?" Jenny asked, startled at the face I made.

"I just got through drinking some of that woman's tea."

She gave me her throaty, grown woman's laugh.

"You're safe enough, I think," she said. "It's not like you're married to her."

Watching Jenny and I caused a flurry of Chinese whispers between Mai and Ayi, followed by some Chinese giggles.

"What did she say?" I asked.

"Ayi told me you sound like her third husband," Mai said.

"How many husbands has she had?"

"Two."

After another bit of a choke, I decided to let that old joke go by.

"I think I need something stronger. Scotch, I think," I said. "You ladies join me?"

Mai and her auntie declined. I poured a couple for Jenny and me.

"My mother used to say…" Jenny took a sip of the Scotch. "Well, first, sit back down."

She patted the couch beside her. I sat, knowing we had come to the heart of the matter of Mrs. Colleta.

"My mother used to say," Jenny continued only after I settled into place beneath the smug gaze of Mai and Ayi. "That if you want to know about a man, look at who he married."

I bet, I thought. "So, you've been around learning all about Donny Colleta. And that helps me how?"

"It gave me a way in. A way to find out about her while people I know thought I wanted to know about him."

"They probably figured you wanted to be his mistress," I said. "Who did you go to for all this asking?"

She gave a shrug and a smile.

"Ladies, society lady types I've met when I worked on stage. Opera and plays. We always hosted audiences after. They seem to want to bask in the glow of show people. As long as none of their children marry us, of course."

"Of course. You know, my mom always said that show people are tacky."

"And gangsters and gamblers are not, I suppose." Jenny bristled.

"Oh no. People like me were hell-bound devil spawn."

"Mrs. Colleta is a fierce woman, Conner. And she's into everything on this Island. Everything civilized anyway."

"What's civilized?" I asked, thinking it was a good question.

"Bunches of charity drives. Funding the city parks. Most of the children's events they hold in them. She heads up committees supporting the town's orphanages and widow's homes…"

"Makes sense," I said, remembering her efforts with Julia, who had a night she barely remembered with the Swede.

"They say no one can pry open a rich man's wallet better than Mrs. Colleta."

"Kind of makes me glad I'm not rich," I said.

"One lady I talked to called her 'the Locomotive,' because of the way she takes on her projects."

"That's something. The Locomotive. I wonder if that's the word Donny uses when he thinks of her."

"Word is, their marriage is a partnership. She shows the same energy and focus in her home and charities that Colleta shows with his businesses."

"Her home, her charities, and, I'm guessing, her place in society?" That was a question. "All this with him being a casino owner?"

"Hmm." Jenny turned pensive and her eyes went here and there into space. "I swear, his casino never came up. Not once. They may not know."

"Smart man."

"Smart woman," Jenny countered. "Among society types, it's a good secret to keep."

A good secret for sure. Anyway, Mr. Colleta's legit businesses kept a good front. I knew he owned a cannery and a marine equipment shop. Some eateries. A couple of these were over on the mainland. There were probably more I didn't remember.

Mai leaned in. "Ayi apologizes, but she would like to know some things."

"Ask your questions, Ayi," I said. I liked the way the old woman's cheeks popped when she gave her shy smile.

So she asked her questions, through Mai, and I stopped liking her old lady cheeks as she did so. The woman wrung me dry. Everything I could remember of those damnable pictures. Everything I could remember of what Doc Kennedy told me about her dying.

Ruined my appetite. Even Jenny turned a pale shade of green.

"I also think Victoria's ghost came for a visit," I ended it, telling about the strange feeling sitting alone in the chair at her house, and the flickering porch light.

Jenny shuddered. Mai smiled. Auntie Ayi sat back, percolated some more nasal crooning, and waved warding signs with her fingers.

"An *égui*. A hungry ghost." Mai translated. "The woman's family must put food out for her. Maybe she goes away in a little while."

I looked at Jenny. "Don't that beat all? A ghost with an empty belly. Who would've thought?"

"Who would have thought that lady's ghost would be blinking at the likes of you, Paddy," Jenny said, chuckling—nervously chuckling.

"Ayi guesses her spirit picked you to placate her," Mai said.

"Is that what she said?" I asked.

Mai's eyes widened, and she put on a smile meant to placate my ghost. "Well, no. But Auntie may have thought of it."

I grinned and shook my head.

Ayi reached a hand to touch Mai's arm. She spoke long and intense and fast to her. Mai seemed to digest what she said before turning to me.

"Ayi says this was more than it seems. More than just poisoning a woman."

"What more?"

"It's punishment, too." Mai said. "A hard death meant to hurt. To shame, even."

A dying meant to hurt and to shame. It seemed like dying was hurt enough. Who'd want the other stuff for Victoria?

Jenny nudged me. "Somebody just pulled up."

Knuckles rapped at the door before I got to it. Victoria's ghost would have to stay hungry.

FIX IT

The man at my door surprised me.

'Froggy' Genova. Froggy because that's what he resembled. Bloat-faced, with full, round jowls that bled from his face seamlessly into a full, round torso, with skinny legs and arms. His watery, bug eyes would fool a fool into thinking he was dumb as that toad he looked like. He was sharp as a tack and smart as a library book. I didn't know all about what he did, but I knew he handled finances for the Beach Gang. I called him Mr. Genova.

He noted the surprise on my mug.

"Yeah, I know. I'm the last guy you'd expect to come to your door," he said. He smiled. A person would know it was a smile even though his slash lips turned down instead of up. "Wha-cha gonna do? Hard to find good help around Christmas."

"Come in," I said.

"Nah. Places to go," he said, then let out a long sigh.

"What?"

"You haven't seen today's paper, huh?"

I shook my head. Genova reached to the over-sized pocket of his flogger. He moved slow. Gangsters always did that slow in case people thought they were going for a gun. I hadn't noticed the folded up newspaper stuffed into it. He handed the paper to me.

"Bottom of page eight," he said. "Buried under the shipping news. Ironic, I thought."

Whatever that meant. The breeze fought me for control of the paper. Took more effort than I'd thought to get it opened to the page and select from three headlines along the bottom.

"Man found beaten?"

"That's the one."

"They don't give his name. But they call him a bootlegger," I said.

"He is that. And his name is Bertie Glazer."

I shook my head. "Don't know him."

"No reason you should. He's Town Gang."

"Why are you bringing this to me?"

"Long story really. But Glazer's saying it's our fault. So the Townies called a big sit down. I just came from there."

"Came or sent?"

"Sent."

"To me?"

"Funny that." He grinned. "Turns out this fool got beat up by a bunch of foreigners."

"Glazer told you this?"

"George Musey did the telling. He's the one that called the sit down."

Ouch. Musey was number three in the Town Gang. A hard-eyed, blood-letting Syrian that had worked with Johnny Jack Nounces for years.

"Don't see the funny part," I said and swallowed hard.

Genova chuckled. "Yep. Funny as hell. It's so funny that Mr. Quinn himself says to get the Irishman out there to fix it. Don't really know what our Irishman, meaning you, had to do with anything, but Mr. Quinn did."

"Fix it?"

"Fix it." Genova held out his hand.

"Fix what?" I asked but got no answer.

"My paper," Genova said, his hand still out.

I had forgotten I still held it. I handed it over. He gave an exasperated growl, made exaggerated efforts to smooth and fold it, then left, tucking it under an arm.

Genova, Genova and Mr. Quinn, boss of the Beach Gang, knew what happened out on the wharf. I did too, damn it.

Three scowling women stared at me when I turned to look back in the house.

"You couldn't pull the door to? The whole winter blew in here," Jenny said.

I barely noticed her. Instead, I went for my coat and hat.

"Mai," I said. "Call Bobbie Lee. I want him and Yuli to meet me at the wharf. Just him and Yuli. Tell him that Dutch stays here."

She looked at me, mystified. The same look in Jenny's eyes, too. Both wanted answers.

"Sure, Conner."

Good. No questions from Mai. Didn't have time for questions.

"Just him and Yuli," I repeated as I went out the door.

Laq stood in the huge emptiness between the last of the warehouses that marked the edge of Galveston city and the tangle of looming cranes serving the piers. Maybe he'd waited for me.

A half-smoked ready-rolled dangled from his lips. One eye squinted, as if the cigarette's smoke burned his eyes. Even though the breeze off the Bay blew the fumes away from his face. Rail thin, and long boned, the Negro stood there, his loose white shirt and brown tweed slacks fluttered. He didn't seem to feel the cold.

"It's about time," he said.

"Yeah, for what?"

Laq eyed me for a couple of seconds. "What did they tell you?"

"I was told to come up here and fix it. Whatever fix it is."

"Anything else?"

"They told me some bum got beat up down here."

"He got beat good, in fact." Laq took the butt from his mouth, but he kept the squint. "Look around. What do you see?"

I saw a port. A busy one, even in midwinter. Some of the cranes swung loads back or forth. Some sort of hulking ship wallowed tied to every pier. A few gulls cried mournful songs. The tang of salt air clashed with smells of fish, and rotting seaweed, and coal burning.

I flashed my palms and shrugged at him.

"What about the men? Look at them," Laq said.

Men loitered about, here and there, in knots. Negro dockworkers for the most part.

"I looked."

"What did you see?" Laq repeated.

"Bunches of men, lounging around and not doin' a lick of work."

"Now why would the Chief allow that to happen?"

By 'the Chief,' Laq meant Chief Higgins, the boss of all the Negro dockworkers and laborers working the wharf. Higgins and I sparred around off and on in the past, but we were mostly friends.

"I was thinking that same thing," I said.

"No you're not, Irish. You're being purposefully obtuse," he slurred. Big words with an accent like the sharecroppers that lived down the highway from my old home.

"I don't know what that is," I said.

"It means you're lying."

"Yeah. You're right." I chinned toward what I knew was Poul's ship. "They're watching the Swedes."

"And why would they be doing that, do you think?"

I'd forgotten my damned gloves, so I slipped my hands into my flogger's pockets and gave Laq a shrug.

"Because they're the ones that beat up the bootlegger."

"Give the bog trotter a Kewpie doll."

"The Swedes didn't even care that they stomped the wrong guy."

Laq shook his head.

"They'll be stomping any bootlegger they find, I'll bet." I said. "Including me, given the chance, I'll bet."

I looked over at the ship then back to Laq.

"So, fix it," he said. The same words Froggy Genova used.

He watched me, his liquid brown eyes rimmed with gold wire glasses.

I let out an exasperated puff of breath and shook my head.

"Yeah. Fix it." I walked past him toward the Swedish ship, and past those knots of dockworkers that cut sideways glances at me.

Not looking at the ship, I followed the line of warehouses waiting for attention. I tried to look like someone who belonged there. Not sure I pulled it off.

Turned out that one of the knots of idle men weren't dockworkers but sailors. I knew them by shags of blond hair beneath their beret-like sailor hats. Well, that and they stood right in front of their ship.

A couple of them eyed me when I turned to them. I ignored them and looked up at the railings of the ship. Four or five officer types, hands held behind them, stood there watching everything.

One of them was Poul. I swiped off my fedora so he'd be sure it was me. He pointed me out then turned and left. The officers stared at me.

Quick enough, Poul quick-stepped down the gangway. He didn't look happy.

Well, I wasn't all that happy either. And not just because the five crewmen on the pier began to follow him.

They all stopped. They weren't looking at me. Yuli and Bobbie Lee had come up from behind me.

A gesture from me made the two of them stop. I took a few steps toward Poul. To my great relief, he gestured to the sailors to stay where they were.

More Swedes, I saw, gathered at the rails by the officers. Reinforcements.

I waited and looked at Poul. It took him about five seconds to begin to walk toward me, but not all the way. He left plenty of room to change his mind—if it needed changing.

"Why are you beating up folks, Poul?" I asked.

"I'm not hurting anyone," he answered.

"Your crew is."

"*Ja, ja.* We Swedes, we protect each other, *ja.*"

"Who were they protecting when they jumped that poor bootlegger?"

Poul's shrug was the kind that told me he'd let the whole thing pass over. "They did not like that you hit me."

"I didn't hit you. And neither did that guy."

"They did not like that your man hit me."

"He wasn't my man," I said, continuing the lie from the afternoon in the deserted warehouse.

"A man of our ship got hit. That is enough for them," he said, sliding from half tenor, half baritone in his strange lilt.

"It's got to stop, Poul," I said. "How can I get it to stop?"

I didn't remind him that, if things didn't stop, the Town Gang would come back here with pistols and all hell would break loose. Maybe they would anyway, if Quinn couldn't get a lid on things. The T-men, and the G-men, and all kinds of men would be crawling all over the wharf. And that wouldn't be good for anybody.

I got another shrug from Poul.

Behind him, the sailors stared at me with their hungry grins. Almost like a gang of schoolboys ready for a fight, poised on the balls of their feet, and some with clinched fists. I'd gotten scrambled good by a bunch like them when I was a kid. And scrambled for less reason. It gave me an idea.

"How about this," I said. "I'll let you take a turn. Hit me."

Well, I thought it was an idea. Might even have worked all those years ago when I got crunched.

Poul looked at me for a moment. "You didn't hit me. You said that."

"Then one of your sailors can hit me. Will that make it good? Will that stop it?"

Poul looked back over his shoulder at the other Swedes, then back at me.

"I must ask them," he said.

At least he considered it.

"Do it then."

One more look at me, as if he weighed how serious I was, before he wandered back to his friends. I was serious enough. Fool me.

Bobbie Lee was beside me. Like magic.

"You're insane," he said.

"They told me to come down here and fix it. I'm down here fixing it. Or trying to," I told him.

"Who told you to do this?"

"Ollie Quinn."

That name stopped Bobbie Lee short.

"Ollie Quinn himself?"

"Well, it was Froggy Genova come to my door," I said. A quick glance back at the Swedes showed them bunched around Poul. I couldn't make out their words but I could make out how angry some of them were.

"Wait," Bobbie Lee said. "Genova climbed out of his lair to run an errand?"

"I wouldn't have believed it either if I hadn't answered the door myself."

Bobbie Lee's eyes drifted up over my shoulder.

"I got your back," he said. "Yuli and me."

I turned. One of the sailors headed up the gangway at a run. The others followed Poul up to me. Close up to me. They had grim, eager smiles, like they had the inside dope on a rigged horse race. Like those bullies back in grade school.

"My crew accepts," Poul said.

"I get punched, and they lay off the Islanders?"

"*Ja. Ja*," he said.

"Which one's gonna do it?" I eyed the men behind him.

"Not these. He comes soon."

Crap. A ringer. Well, Dutch was sort of my ringer the day we'd ambushed Poul. My stomach went cold and I questioned certain of my life choices.

The Swede that came down the gangway looked like a circus freak. Short and squat, but not fat. He seemed like he was mostly shoulders. Huge shoulders jutting out from his neck. Not only did he have wildly bowed legs but his arms bowed out from his torso like he carried a huge invisible hoop. A flattened nose, a sun-creased and pitted face the color of old newspaper decorated a skull too small for the rest of him. And he wasn't all that big a guy.

He came up to Poul with the same evil, hungry grin the others wore.

Poul and the guy exchanged hard-chewed and half-sung Swedish with Poul making gestures toward me while the guy made sidelong glances at me. I guessed he had lots of questions.

Finally, he nodded. He looked way too eager.

I put up my hand, "One punch, just like you. Tell him that. One punch."

"And not in the face," Bobbie Lee put in. I thanked him silently.

"Tell him," I repeated.

Well, Poul told him something and the man nodded again. He squared off on me.

A gut punch was coming my way. I took a half step back to brace up. And, as any man would do, expecting what I expected, I clinched my guts as hard as I could.

The man's fist went back, but it did not come up toward my stomach. That bowed-up arm came in from the side, with the speed of a crashing plane, into the left side of my ribcage.

I felt like I'd been kicked by a mule. I thought I heard the echo of it bounce off the walls of the warehouses. Still, I kept my feet under me. Barely.

It didn't knock the wind out of me. Not much anyway.

"Okay," I managed to grunt. "We're good? We're done, right?"

Poul turned his head to speak more Swedish to the sailors behind him.

"*Ja,*" he said to me.

"No more bootleggers gonna get beaten up?" This was a raspy whisper.

"*Ja.* No more," he said.

I turned, limped away panting, and did not look back.

Bobbie Lee and Yuli sidled up on either side of me. Both their heads swirled, glancing at me, glancing at each other, and glancing back behind us. Concerned about me and concerned about being followed.

I saw a couple of the dock workers that had gathered for the show shoot me some looks, but otherwise, I just stared straight ahead. It was over.

Well, mostly.

Just about three steps away from the Studebaker and the sneeze happened. Not a sneeze, *the sneeze.*

The sneeze and the loud pop like a dry limb busted in two.

"Holy God, was that you?" Bobbie Lee asked grabbing a hold of me as I grabbed my ribcage.

Not kicked this time, I felt like I'd been shot. I could only nod.

"Give me the keys. I'm taking you to Doc Kennedy."

"Bobbie Lee is right, you know. You are insane," Jenny said.

She'd come out of the bathroom, still toweling her hair, after trying to wash off the smell of cigar smoke. Her wooly sox warmed her feet and one of my shirts covered her body, opened at the throat and showing her long legs. As far as I could tell, she wore nothing else. She looked good.

"I told you so. Didn't I tell you?" Bobbie Lee said.

He'd been necking with Mai since the last mark left. They sat locked together on the couch. It surprised me that he pried his lips off her long enough to comment.

I ignored both comments. They'd been said all too often since I got back from Doc Kennedy.

"Aren't you cold?" I asked Jenny as she sat by me at my new poker table.

"Aren't you sleepy?" she asked in return. "You're full of Doc's pain pills."

"Sleepy as hell, but that crap makes me restless."

"You hurting?" She reached to run a finger down the webbed shoulder strap beneath the shirt I wore. She ended it with a gentle poke at the laces giving tension to the canvas rib brace. "Does it help?"

I shrugged.

"How long do you have to wear it?"

"Doc said six weeks," Bobbie Lee told her.

Maybe not that long, I thought to myself. No way I would say that to these three. They were having way too much fun mothering me.

"Maybe it'll remind you how insane you are." Jenny pushed that finger into my stomach, below the edge of the brace. "I can't believe you stood there and let those men crack your ribs. How did you dream that up?"

"Look, ya'll," I said to all three of them. "Those fools were a bunch of over-grown kids. They got all excited—like a bunch of dumb kids. If they kept it up, our Down Town friends were gonna go to the pier and shoot a bunch of them. And all because I roughed up one of their guys."

Jenny laid a hand up on my scratchy, unshaven cheek. "And you think it'll work."

A statement, not a question.

"It couldn't hurt. I hope. Anyway, I figured Mr. Quinn, Froggy, and others are still trying to keep a lid on things. Blood spilled will get all the wrong kinds of attention."

"Do they know what you did down there?" Mai asked.

I chuckled. It hurt. "By now they ought to. Forty people, at least, caught my act."

"Strange kind of solitaire you're playing," Jenny said and pointed at the three cards on the table in front of me.

"I'm running my own poker game. These are my marks."

"The King of Diamonds. The Queen of Spades. The Jack of Clubs," she said. I nodded. "Let me guess. The King's your sailor. The Queen's Mrs. Colleta. And the Jack is the slug."

"You got it."

"And the point?"

"Just trying to see which one of them's having any luck,"

"I know about twenty ways to tell a fortune with a deck of cards, Conner."

Telling me their future, I thought to myself. I didn't really want her to know, but I might be their future, in ways they wouldn't like. At least for one of the three.

"Not sure I want to know about their futures." I dealt a hand in front of each of the three face cards.

Jenny leaned forward to prop herself on her elbows. "Three sevens for the Queen."

"Yeah. The woman's on a run,"

"Is that significant?" she asked.

I didn't know one way or another, so I shrugged.

"You got any luck running for yourself tonight, Irish?"

The mischievous glint in her eyes was heavy with hidden meaning. Meaning I picked up easily enough.

"Geez," I rubbed at the brace under my shirt. "If a man's gotta work to make his own luck, I don't know how much I can work up."

"Let me do most of the work," she breathed into my ear.

"Bobbie Lee, lock up for me," I called out. "But I want you, Dutch, and Yuli here tomorrow."

He gave me a look as full of meaning as Jenny had. A different sort of meaning. He was as good as Jenny at reading me. Maybe better.

"Tell me when," he said.

"As soon as you can wake them up."

I watched Jenny and Mai exchange glances. They'd have to puzzle things out on their own.

Jenny took my hand and led me down the hall. Where she did most of the work.

FIVE BULLETS

---◦✦◦---

"This is who you picked?" Bobbie Lee asked as he leaned back against the Studebaker's door. Behind him, the drizzle made sad runnels down the window.

Behind us, Dutch and Yuli filled the back seat. All three looked at me.

"I didn't pick nothing. This is who did it."

That's what I said. In truth, I only had a gut feeling on it. Like I was God or something.

"Why not the other one?" Dutch asked.

"Or that rich woman?" Yuli put in. Like Bobbie Lee, he always believed what Mai believed.

"Her," I said. "As far as I could see, that woman is a queen. She rules her own little island empire. She clears her throat and people start bowing. Her husband might be a help. But I'd lay odds that the man gets in her way as much as anything else. A woman like Victoria, or ten women, would just keep him out of her hair."

"So you think she's better alive and kicking than dead and cold to Mrs. Colleta, huh?" Bobbie Lee said.

"Yep. That's the way I see it."

It sounded more right when I said it out loud.

Bobbie Lee folded his arms across his chest. "I figured you'd go for the sailor."

"Because he got my rib broke."

"That'd be reason enough for me," he said.

"I guess it would be—for you. Maybe even for me on a different day," I said. "But it won't be for Mr. Colleta."

"Ribs or not, the sailor could've done it."

"He didn't."

"Why not?" Bobbie Lee asked.

"Because he didn't kill that girl in that hotel room," I explained. "I didn't get the idea that good ol' Poul liked his women dead."

"So that leaves the slug, Harold," Bobbie Lee said.

"That leaves the slug," I agreed. I hoped I was right.

New, heavy rain started thudding on the Studebaker's canvas roof, as if to tell my crew that that might not be the truth.

"What the hell," Dutch said. "We scoop him up, drag him to Colleta, and get our butts home."

Bobbie Lee read the grimace squeezing at my eyes.

"It might turn out different than that, Dutch," he said, dousing the back of the car into silence. Like always, my friend read me like a book.

I scratched the shave-raw skin of my chin. Time to say something.

"It might, boys," I said. "I guess you need to choose. Bail out of here now. No hard feelings. But if you go with me and the thing goes sideways, there will be no turning back."

I laid that raw chin of mine down on my arm propped over the top of my seat. Doing it hurt my ribs. I watched the wheels turn in the skulls of the two men.

Yuli spoke first. Strangely, I knew he would.

"I belong. I go with you," he said.

"I have to ask, Conner, why are we just now hearing this?" Of the two of them, Dutch was the man that thought things out.

Bobbie Lee chuckled. "That's because there was nothing to tell afore now. I suspect Conner's just now hearing this, same as you."

I shot him a flare of a glance despite him being right.

"The first thing I'm gonna do is to get the truth out of him," I said. "Not really sure how he's gonna take it."

"So, Dutch, you coming?" Bobbie Lee grinned.

"Of course. Like Yuli said, we're crew. I'm crew."

Bobbie Lee clenched a fist and gave it a shake. Affirmation. I thought he was as grateful as I that my crew was solid together in this. That made this something I had to get right.

I took a breath. A shallow one. Taking a deep one hurt even if the rib brace allowed one.

"Let's do it then," I said.

I'd parked the Studebaker around the block from Harold's house—away from any snooping eyes. Under that same tree where I'd left Bobbie Lee the day he'd broken into it. Rain fell that day as well.

To spite my fedora and the turned up collar of my flogger, the rain got on my neck and down the back of my shirt. Cold rain that drew up the skin between my shoulder blades.

Four men couldn't find a way to stroll down a street. Not in the winter. Not sopping wet. Couldn't keep it down to a stroll. We didn't exactly run but we certainly quick-marched. What a damn parade it was.

I kept swiveling neck and eyes. I even sniffed for smells. All drapes were drawn. To hold in the heat, I guessed. Chimneys smoked, mostly sour coal smoke that mixed with the smells off the bay. Dead fish, rotting seaweed, salt water brought in on the North wind.

Maybe we weren't noticed.

"There it is," I pointed to the house with the neat but winter-burned yard and the need for some new paint. It too puffed smoke from its chimney.

"What do you want us to do?" Dutch asked.

Well, I had kind of a plan.

"Yuli, you're carrying, right?"

"Always." He patted the pistol he kept in his heavy pea coat.

"Go around back. Don't sneak. Look like you belong back there," I said. "The rest of us'll just go in the front door. Dutch, you last. Stay by the door. Nobody leaves the house."

"What if he don't invite us in?" Dutch asked. Always thinking, that Dutch.

Bobbie Lee filched a flask from his hip pocket. "Offer him a pull on this and act insulted if he won't do it."

"Let's hope I don't have to force my way in," I said.

Dutch settled himself in my wake as Yuli split off to head around the back of the house. His scuffed boots squelched on the wet, yellow grass.

"What do you want from me?" Bobbie Lee whispered. Hard to hear through the hissing rain.

I thought about it a couple of seconds.

"If we're in easy, be silent and pretend you want to kill him. I'll do a flimflam."

"I won't be pretending, Conner."

I tried not to make too much noise climbing Harold's steps. Bobbie Lee clattered like a new pony and Dutch thumped up like the pony's mother. I shook my head, took a breath—again—and started slapping the door with the flat of my hand.

Harold took his time getting to the door. He stared, disheveled, and greasy. Angry eyes.

I shouldered in past him before he could say anything. Before he could push the door closed in my face.

"What's up, Buttercup," I said, shaking and stomping as much rain water as possible over as much of the entry as possible.

Bobbie Lee and Dutch pressed in behind me and did the same thing. Harold had to step back from Dutch as the big blond freed the door from his grasp and closed it.

"It's kind of early," Harold protested. He stood barefooted, in an A-shirt and rumpled, tan slacks. Over the clutter that stank of stale cigar smoke, spilled beer, and soured carpet, he smelled three days sweaty.

"To you, early. To us, late. We ran out of places to go drinkin'," I grinned. A lie on the fly.

Bobbie Lee took a pull from his flask to back my story. However, he kept a scowl on his baby face.

I didn't think Harold bought the story. But we were in and Dutch stood in front of the door. His huge frame almost hid the damn thing.

I took off my flogger and hung it on the worn coatrack. It swayed, unsteady.

My grin faded. I faced him and tried to loom. Not too hard. I was tall and he wasn't.

Harold wouldn't look me in the eye.

"What are you here for?" he asked.

"Yeah. You're right. It's not the truth."

"What do you want?" He grew smaller, if that was possible.

"We want you to pay your debt," I said.

"I don't owe you anything," Harold protested. He even looked like he had a spine—for a moment.

"You owe me, little man," Bobbie Lee said, though he wasn't all that much bigger than Harold. "You owe me for the murder of Victoria Yeats."

"He's here to shoot you dead, Harold," I said.

I watched the color leave his face. For two long seconds he stood stock still. Then he bolted. And the three of us stood stock still.

His bare feet slapping the floor as he fled to the back of the house was almost funny.

Harold came to a dead stop at the back door. Then he was backing up, Yuli's gat pressed to his forehead.

"Sit down, Harold," I said when he backed up to the soiled, dark olive couch.

Yuli's other hand gave him a gentle push. He plopped down. His stunned expression turned into a desperate protest.

"I didn't do it."

"That's a shame, boy, because you're gonna die for it," I assured him.

He turned to Bobbie Lee and opened his jaw to speak.

"Put a cork in it, you slug. I been paid. You're done." Funny how Bobbie Lee's innocent, beardless, young face could look snake evil when he wanted to.

"Please, man. Please. I got money," Harold begged.

Bobbie Lee pretended to consider that for a minute.

"You gotta wad, huh?" Bobbie Lee asked.

Harold nodded.

"Where is it?" Show me?"

Desperation passed over Harold's face.

"Well, I don't have it here. I mean, it's in the bank and stuff."

"Hear that?" Bobbie Lee asked the room. "The fool don't have two nickels to rub together."

"I do. I swear. Just not here. I can get it. I just need time. Please," Harold began to sweat.

"The time is now, man."

Bobbie Lee reached into the pocket of his flogger.

"Please, God. Please. I'll do anything. I'll give you everything I have. Please." Tears rolled down his face.

Bobbie Lee just shook his head. He even scared me.

Harold turned his wide eyes in my direction.

"Please. Give me a chance, Gambler. Just give me a chance."

My guts got all knotty as I looked down at him. The smell of his fear had gotten louder than the smell of his filth and sweat. A metallic tang on top of the goaty musk. And the bastard called me Gambler. Damn it to hell.

I fished my own revolver from where I'd tucked it behind me, stuck in my belt.

Harold made a squeaking noise. He made to beg again but I flashed the palm of my other hand.

I thumbed back the pistol's hammer to half cock, then thumbed back the latch so the cylinder opened with a push from my forefinger. Looking at Harold, not at the Colt, my left hand started slow, purposeful movements to pick the bullets from their chambers one at a time.

"I guess I am a gambler, Harold…"

"What gives?" Bobbie Lee barked. I shook my head surreptitiously and shot him a glare.

"So I'll give you a chance to gamble on your life." I held out my hand. "Here. Five bullets. Five out of six. Good odds."

I put the five bullets in my shirt pocket and closed the cylinder as Harold watched.

"What if he loses?" Dutch asked. Not always the sharpest penny, was Dutch.

"Then it won't matter, will it?"

With the hammer still at half-cock, I gave the cylinder a spin.

"Hey, man, I'm on the job here," Bobbie played along. Made me proud.

"If you live, Harold, I won't let the man kill you. Good deal, huh? I'll want something though. I'll want you to tell me the truth. If you don't, the deals off. You hear?"

Maybe he did.

I spun the cylinder again and pushed the pistol barrel against his temple. He flinched away from it but I followed him as he folded across the couch.

I pulled the hammer all the way. Full cock. Harold let out a sob.

The Colt clicked when I squeezed the trigger. Harold's sob turned into panting cries.

"Jesus bleeding Christ, Conner," Dutch called out. I regretted him using my real name.

Bobbie Lee laughed. "Jesus had nothing to do with it. Neither did any odds."

"What?" Dutch asked.

"My superstitious Irish friend don't do odds. The big chicken's always afraid his gat'll go off and blow his tackle all to hell. Only keeps five pills in the thing. Keeps the hammer against the one empty chamber." Bobbie Lee shook his head.

Harold screamed out. "You fuck. You bastard," he cursed.

"Screw it, man," I said. "Now tell me. You couldn't have her so you made sure no one else could either, right?"

He said nothing. He just kept panting. Noisy, explosive breaths.

I shrugged, popped the Colt's cylinder opened, pulled the bullets from my pocket, and started to reload. I guess Harold got the idea.

"That's not it. You don't understand, goddammit," he managed.

"So make me understand," I said. He looked at Bobbie Lee, fear in his eyes. "Tell me. I won't let him kill you. Not if you tell me."

"I do have her. I took her. She's mine. Forever."

"She's dead, man," Bobbie Lee said.

"She's in hell. She waits for me there."

I just about let out my own sob. Bobbie Lee's jaw dropped.

Victoria Yeats' image flashed before my eyes. That picture of her with her husband. That happy, world-by-the-tail smile. Full of life. Deserving life. Christ on a crutch, what a mess. My mess.

I stepped over to the rickety coatrack and threw the flogger over my arm.

"You can't leave it like this, Conner," Bobbie Lee sounded like he begged.

I ignored him and turned to Harold. My hand still held the Colt.

"Donny Colleta," I said to him.

"Who?" Harold asked.

"Donny Colleta. He's the rich man that had Victoria. She was never yours, Harold. Never will be. Not even in hell."

I thumbed back the Colt's hammer again, pointed it at Harold's forehead, and pulled the trigger.

Despite the muffling provided by the flogger, it was the loudest pistol shot I had ever heard. It was the loudest shot I would ever hear.

THE STATION

A guy ought to feel something when he kills a man. I felt empty, like a flat tire. Bobbie Lee and the others cringed away from the bloody mess that used to be Harold.

An eerie, electrified fluttering ran up and down my skin. But I just stood there, dumb and useless.

Bobbie Lee's hand on my arm brought me out of it—a little.

"You all right?" he asked, his eyes worried for me.

"He called me Gambler," is what came into my mind to say.

Bobbie Lee reached up to scratch his lower lip, puzzled. He must have realized how worthless I was at that moment. He took over.

"Dutch, peek out the front. See if anybody's showing any interest," he ordered.

"Got it."

"Yuli, this place needs to burn. Sometime after we're gone, if we can manage it."

Yuli grinned. A big grin. "Ha, that I can do."

He rushed to the kitchen and started a noisy, clattering search.

Bobbie Lee touched my arm again.

"You didn't have to do it, Conner. I'd a done him."

I stirred my tongue around to put some spit back in my mouth.

"It's my mess, not yours. But thanks anyway." I said hoarsely.

My crew must've been busy. I looked at the wall until Bobbie Lee turned me by the elbow and gave me a little push toward the door. We left behind the sulfur smell of a struck match and of burnt candle wax. Bobbie Lee's eyes showed he worried about me, but I made him give me the keys to the car anyway. It had stopped raining.

The mess was still a mess. My crew didn't know that, I figured. I drove Yuli and Dutch to their rooming house over off 31st Street.

"Stay close to home for a while," Bobbie Lee urged, as they closed the doors. They must have made some faces at him. "He's all right."

Was I?

I drove him to Mai's place. A cozy little bungalow filled with her entire family, if the passel of bundled-up kids and a squad of ancient grannies on the porch was any indication. It probably hadn't been painted since Noah got off the ark. Two near-new Cadillacs and a shiny Nash parked in front, however.

Bobbie Lee shot me a face as he climbed out of the Studebaker. Maybe the same questioning expression as the other two.

"He called me Gambler." I said.

He didn't know it, but that was the answer to everything that day.

There was stuff to do. I just hadn't figured out what.

After an hour or two of driving around thinking about it, the least of the worst choices required something from a dangerous man. I chose it anyway—there were no good choices.

If it worked, I might be able to live with myself. Even get away with it.

Sooner than I wanted, I stood before Sam Maceo.

We met in an office of the Chop Suey Café, the opulent cabaret built out over the Gulf on a pier, just across Seawall Boulevard from the equally grand Galvez Hotel. I felt the tender shudder made from waves pounding the pier's pilings. Distant, hollow music played somewhere farther down the structure. Off and on, an orchestra rehearsing, practicing for the New Year's Eve gala I knew was coming.

Mr. Maceo, brother of my boss, Rose Maceo, relaxed behind an ornate mahogany desk. Wavy hair, perfect. Silk suit, immaculate. Expression, calm. His glittering eyes weighed me thoroughly.

"You look frayed and worn, Conner," he said.

Made me feel like a winter-bit thorn bush. "I apologize for my appearance, Mr. Maceo."

He shrugged the shrug I'd expect from a Prussian prince.

"Lily said that seeing me was important to you," he said.

"She did?" I wondered what gave me away.

"A talent much appreciated here." He gave me his million dollar smile. The smile he was already famous for. "Is it? Important to you, I mean."

"To me it is."

Mr. Maceo sat back, looking regal but more distant. "Speak, Conner."

"I need a favor, sir." I sat. But I felt shabby.

His eyes sparkled though he didn't change expression.

"My favors can be expensive."

Crap. I thought a moment.

"I don't have much money, but I do have one thing," I ventured. I had other uses for that money in my pocket. He waited. "A favor for a favor."

"A favor for a favor," he seemed to consider that. "What do you want?"

So I told him. I kept it brief and left out everything that had happened that day.

He paused and I felt sweat under my wet clothes. Then, despite the inkpot and pen set between him and I, he took up a pencil from a cup. I guessed he let others chance ink stained fingers. The pencil scratched on a piece of note paper. He folded it once.

I had to stand to get it from his hand when he held it out.

"You'll hear from me." Mr. Maceo smiled.

Christ on the cross, I owed Sam Maceo a favor.

That did nothing to calm anything. My skin still crawled. My belly still churned. My soul wanted a stiff drink. The Studebaker took me home—or seemed to.

Being early, the place was empty. I was glad.

I had driven a nail, at a slant, into the inside header of my bedroom closet. A person would have to enter the closet, turn around, and look up to see it. A folded wad of paper money was wedged behind it. My get away stash in case I had to lam.

For the first time, as I stuffed the money into the flogger's pocket, I noticed the gun powder burns on it. Scorch marks on the right sleeve and on the side, near the buttons. Where the gun was when I squeezed the trigger.

Nothing to do about it. Didn't have another one.

The walk to the kitchen, to the phone, felt long for some reason. The operator got Windy's phone ringing.

"We're going out," I said. Blunt, even rash. "Dress warm."

"Conner, Harold's house is on fire," she said, ignoring what I'd said.

"It is?" Good to know. Whatever Yuli did must've worked. "Is he all right?"

A gangster's life is full of lies.

"I wouldn't know. I haven't seen him. But the whole neighborhood smells," she said.

"I'll get you away from it, then," I said, then repeated. "Dress warm."

"Maybe he'll come by," she said.

"Then we'll take him with us," I said. Lie upon lie.

The kitchen door cracked open. Jenny's face peeked through. I put a finger to my lips, so she wouldn't talk—I hoped.

"Where we going?" Windy asked, her voice buzzy in the receiver.

"I don't know. Downtown." Only half a lie. "I'm leaving now. Be ready."

"I'll be ready."

I hung up.

Jenny arched an eyebrow at me. Puzzled and maybe angry.

"I'll be back when I can," I told her and gave her a kiss on her mouth. That left her surprised as well. I didn't think she noticed the burnt patches on my coat.

The fire still burned at Harold's. The whole neighborhood stank of it, just as Windy said.

Windy met me at her door, showing those wide, warm eyes. She took me at my word and dressed in tan wool, with stockings to match.

Not like Jenny, she noticed my ruined coat.

"Are you all right, Conner?" she asked, closing the door.

I was not in the mood to say one way or the other.

"You need to pack a bag."

"Are you whisking me away?" she teased.

"You have to leave, Windy." I said.

"I don't understand." She reacted to the look on my face, it seemed.

"He called me Gambler, Windy."

"Who called you that?"

"Harold did."

"So? I mean—I mean—well, what do you mean?"

"At first I thought it meant that you only talked to the fool about me," I said. "But I've been wondering about the coffee table that got moved."

"Moved?"

"One side set forward, up next to the chair—also moved." That was the way I'd found it when I first went to Victoria's house. The way I saw it in Doc Kennedy's crime photos. "At first I figured he moved it to put a drink on it or something. While he watched Victoria die…"

"He probably did, Conner." Was she suddenly defensive? Maybe.

"No. I figure you probably drug it over to sit beside him. You helped him kill her. You watched with him."

"I can't believe you think that," she protested. Fear entered her eyes, and I knew I was right.

"You and I both know it's true. You wanted the house. Or, maybe you just didn't like her," I said. "Harold wasn't smart enough to do this on his own."

Windy fired up, angry. Possibly desperate. "You're not even asking me if I did it. Don't you even want to ask me?"

Not even a bit interested in hearing *her* lies.

"What I want doesn't matter a bit. If I can figure it out, others can. You stay in town, somebody's gonna kill you."

I left out the fact that I'd be the one to do it.

"Ask me, damn it!" Windy went on. She wasn't quite as pretty anymore.

"I won't, Windy. That's a question you should never answer. Ever."

She got this strange look on her face. Like she was considering, adding something up maybe.

"I didn't watch Victoria. I watched Harold." She sighed. An angry sigh. "Men are such beasts. The look on his face. Like my dog watching me fry eggs. He looked... He got..."

"Aroused?"

She nodded. "You are wrong, you know. He was smart enough on his own. He staged this whole thing, like one of my father's plays."

"Where did y'all get the poison?"

"We—he made it."

I didn't miss the "we" she started with.

"Rat poison from his garden shed," I said.

Windy nodded. "Some cocaine, too. And some crushed cherry pits, if you can believe it. Who knew cherry pits were poisonous. We poured it in some nasty bootlegged whiskey."

"Christ in a truck, woman!" And I worried about Mai's auntie's tea. "I've got to get you out of town."

"You're scaring me."

"Good. You need to be scared." I nodded.

"Where can I go?" Finally, Windy picked up on how things were.

"To the train station. I got you tickets west." I patted at my breast pocket. Those I'd picked up after seeing Mr. Maceo. "Try to hurry. I figure Harold's in that burning house. If he said anything to whoever..."

No sense in letting her know that was me as well.

Windy let out a filthy curse and lit out to the back of her house.

Sooner than I hoped, the two of us were on the station's concourse. The burning sulfur smells around her house were exchanged for the smells of hot metal and steam.

Half-hidden by her cloche hat and the fox fur trim of her heavy coat, the fool girl looked worried. I turned her to me and lifted her chin with a finger, until she looked at me.

"Here," I said reaching into my flogger to remove things from my jacket pocket. I handed her a packet. "These are your tickets. They'll get you all the way to Los Angeles."

She took them, with puzzled eyes.

"Here's a name," I handed her the paper that Sam Maceo gave me. "This man will get you work in the movies. You're born for that, I think. Mention Sam Maceo's name."

The favor for a favor from the man.

Windy mumbled her thanks.

"Some money. All I could get," I said, fishing my wad from the flogger. "Enough to keep you a few months, if you take care."

"Is there no other way?" she asked.

I shook my head. "Don't know of any."

She stared at me.

"Don't come back here. I want you safe." I nodded again.

"But my belongings? All my stuff?"

"Send for it. Get your parents to pack it up."

"I don't want to go."

"Better to go and live than stay."

Windy looked helpless and drawn in. Smaller than she was. But, finally, she nodded.

"Thank you, Conner. For all this."

"I want you safe." I shrugged. I didn't want to be the one to clean up this last part of my mess, either.

I picked up her suitcase, a nice one, leather, almost never used. We walked to her train car. And I walked along its flank, watching through the windows until I saw her take a seat. She didn't look at me, or anything else but the back of the seat in front of her.

The train chugged and puffed its way out of the station, with me standing there.

ABOUT THE AUTHOR

Steven D. Malone received a BA in History from the University of Houston. He has been a teacher of life skills and work skills to special needs students, adjudicated youth, and the visually impaired as well as College English. He is a published author whose works have been featured in venues as diverse as *True West Magazine*, and *KOL Israel Radio*. He is the author of the historical fiction and historical mystery novels: *Sideshow at Honey Creek*, *Southing*, and *Murder in the Brothel Garden*.

He says of himself: I am a voracious reader of anything from historical fiction to cosmology to the backs of cereal boxes. My interests include ancient and Dark Age history, the Civil War and the American West, Taoist and Buddhist philosophy, and classic movies. I am also a certified teacher of Tajiquan. In my life I have been a drifter, a construction worker, a beach bum, a library page, a book store clerk, a teacher, and a writer. Presently, I am a happy husband and a proud father of son and two cats.

Visit the author at his website: www.stevenspen.com

Mr. Malone also asks that you take the time to write a review of the book on Amazon and Goodreads.

www.ingramcontent.com/pod-product-compliance
Lightning Source LLC
Chambersburg PA
CBHW030956210726
48290CB00007B/2330